Duel in the High Hills

Lothrop, Lee &
Shepard Co. / New York

Weekly Reader Children's Book Club
presents

Duel in the High Hills

Arthur Catherall

Contents

1
Four-footed Killer

TEMBA SAW THE ANIMAL FIRST. GLANCING UP AT A steep slope a quarter of a mile away, as he beat the snow from his fur cap, the thirteen-year-old noticed a movement. Turning, he called to his father, who was knocking snow off the baskets strung across the backs of their caravan of sheep and goats.

"Father, look, is that a snow leopard? Over there. Stalking one of the wild blue sheep, the *bharal*."

Shainu Droma snarled a command to one of their three wolflike dogs. He did not look around until the dog, obeying him, had hustled back into the flock a big billy goat that had wandered off in the hope of finding food. Then the thickset hillman turned to stare across the slope. He gave a grunt of disgust.

"Yes, my son, it is a snow leopard, the curse of all who travel these hills."

While their flock of heavily ladened sheep and goats nosed at the melting snow in the hope of finding a few blades of spring grass, Temba and his father watched the four-footed hunter. There was no doubt that she was a snow leopard, for her pale gold hide was dotted with black rosettes, the identifying mark of her kind.

A dozen of the *bharal,* which roam the Himalayan hills, were grazing the slope, and the snow leopard had stalked one so well that she had not only got above it but between it and the rest of the flock as well. Unaware that sudden death was less than ten yards away, the sheep dug into the snow to crop the pale green grass.

Suddenly the snow leopard came out into the open. A magnificent bound carried her to within ten feet of the sheep. Another leap should have seen the kill, but with a terrified bleat the sheep started to run. As the leopard began her second leap something went wrong. A stone twisted under her paws and instead of making another great bound the spotted hunter pitched onto her nose and rolled over. By the time she was up, the blue sheep had a lead of twenty yards and the rest of the flock had joined in the flight.

"Hurt a foreleg," Shainu Droma growled. He slipped the protecting rag cover from the muzzle of his rifle, then pushed it back again, grunting, "Too far to risk a bullet."

"But we could get to her, Father," Temba urged. His eyes were alight at the thought of a snow-leopard pelt. "We——" And there his father stopped him.

"You have a lot to learn, my son," Shainu Droma told him. "Hurt she may be, but once we move she will see us and, injured leg or no injured leg, she will vanish.

By the look of her, she has kittens somewhere, and for courage and devilish cunning, few things can match a snow leopard when she has young."

"How do you know she has young?" Temba asked, wondering at his father's knowledge.

"She is thin," Shainu explained. "That means she is feeding two or three kittens. And a mother snow leopard is worse than any other. Come . . . we have wasted enough time. Tonight we must build a big fire. If that leopard is hungry, she will hear our sheep and goats . . . and she might pay us a visit."

Shainu pulled on his fur cap and turned to look back at the way they had come. For forty years he had been crossing the fourteen-thousand-foot pass that led from his home country of Bhutan to the warmer lowlands of northern India; but he had seldom known a crossing such as the one he and Temba had just made. For four days they had trudged through fierce winds that had whipped up a blinding mist of fine snow. At night in the little tent in which they had slept a thermometer would have registered thirty degrees below zero.

He called to the dogs, and the caravan headed down the rocky trail. Two hours later the lead goat broke the silence with a glad bleating, and Shainu Droma blew out a great sigh of relief. The goat turned off the track, and came to a flat, open space, the only one for miles about. The rest of the tired flock joined in the joyful bleating and hurried after their leader.

"How do they know where to stop?" Temba asked as he followed his father and the dogs. Below them, on the plateau, was a rough stone compound, with a stone fireplace in the center.

His father laughed softly. "Goats and sheep may seem stupid, my son, but they do not forget the important things of life. Like us, they have been four days crossing that ·accursed pass. But for them there has been a difference: while we slept in a tent, they huddled together in the wind and the snow. The older ones remember where there is shelter. Next year the younger ones also will remember."

Temba nodded. He knocked his felt-booted feet against a stone to try to bring some warmth to them. Since he wore no gloves, he kept his hands warm by drawing them up inside his long sleeves. Though still only a boy, Temba showed signs of growing up to be as tough and durable as his father. In this wild country there were neither doctors nor medicines, and the weak died early.

While his father took a bundle of twigs from a pannier, an arrangement of baskets slung over the back of each sheep and goat, Temba closed the entrance to the compound. This "gate" was a bundle of thorny branches left by previous travelers.

"Give the flock some hay," his father ordered. "Not too much, for tomorrow we should be down where there is good grass and where they can drink at a stream."

Temba began to unsaddle the flock. Both goats and sheep carried panniers that held bundles of tightly packed yaks' tails or musk oil, bags of salt, of borax, or of *lac,* a resinous substance much prized by lowland merchants for the making of dyes. As Temba relieved each animal of its burden it rolled over and over to scratch its back on the rocky ground. By the time Temba had stacked the last of the bundles, the flock was waiting patiently. The animals knew which bales contained the sweet-scented mountain hay, and they surged forward, baaing and bleating as he cut the cords binding the first bale.

Shainu had started the fire. As the flames began to leap, he filled one of their cooking pots with snow from a corner of the compound. But before putting the pot on the fire, he took from his coat pocket a small tea brick. It was almost as hard as stone, but it would soften and break apart before the water began to boil.

"What will Mother and Sister be doing now?" Temba asked as he finished spreading the hay so that each of the flock would have an equal chance of getting a full belly.

"Since it is time to eat they will be doing the same thing we are doing," his father said. "Your mother will be making a meal. I am beginning to think that when she cut her leg and had to stay behind, she was lucky. She and your sister have missed the bad weather. I have never known so much wind and snow so late in the spring." Then, as he saw his son standing idle, he said curtly, "Cut up the half sheep, or we shall never eat, and I am hungry."

"I was sorry for my sister," Temba murmured, picking up part of a sheep they had butchered three days earlier. "She cried when she could not come with us."

His father merely grunted, and once again looked

back the way they had come. It had been a hard trek from the upland valleys of Bhutan, but the worst was over. They were now eight thousand feet lower down than they had been the previous night. Here there was no howling wind, and he decided not to pitch their black tent. A night in the open would not harm them.

Temba handed the first piece of mutton he had hacked from the half-frozen carcass to his father, and Shainu dropped it with a *plop* into another cooking pot.

When the pot was half full, he carried it across to the bank of snow, taking his rifle with him. In these wild hills a man's best friend was often his rifle, and Shainu Droma slept with his gun by his side.

It was a splendid weapon. It had been stolen from a British soldier, then sold to first one man and then another before coming into Shainu's hands. He kept it clean, polished, and well oiled. He had even hammered silver nails into the butt for decoration. When he died the Lee-Enfield rifle would become Temba's property, and later, in turn, it would be passed on to his son.

Shainu put the mutton pot well into the fire, added more twigs, then crouched there, warming his hands and waiting. When both pots were beginning to bubble he added a small piece of butter to the tea to improve its flavor. The Bhutanese never use sugar, and the milk they get from the sheep and goats they make into cheese.

Finally Shainu tossed a handful of barley meal into the mutton pot, turning to cuff one of the fierce-looking dogs that had come a little too near. The mastiffs were more like wolves than dogs and knew more of kicks and cuffs than petting. They were watching their master now, tongues lolling and eyes like emeralds. The dogs had not eaten since the previous evening and were ravenous. And except for their breakfast of mugs of black tea thickened with barley meal, neither had Shainu and Temba eaten since the previous night.

Although Temba was hungry, he sat without speaking until his father dug his big knife into the pot. Bringing out a piece of steaming mutton, he held it up and let some of the barley-thickened soup drip onto his tongue. The eyes of the three mastiffs shone even brighter green. Every muscle tense, they inched forward, hoping that the piece of mutton would be tossed to them, a prize for the quickest to snap.

Shainu bit off a piece of the mutton. He was just about to nod to his son as a sign that the meal was ready when, silently as a ghost, a firelit shape appeared on top of the compound wall. It was the snow leopard. She remained there without sound or movement. She was starvation hungry, but the sight of two humans, three dogs, and the leaping flames made her hesitate. Then the scent of sheep and goats overcame her fear and she tensed for a leap. Shainu Droma was tossing the test piece of mutton to his dogs, chuckling as, in a snarling fury, the dogs pounced. At the same time the snow leopard leaped. She seemed to float off the top of the wall, a firelit pale golden shape, long and sinewy. The sheep and goats had finished their hay and were huddled together. They saw nothing and heard nothing until the snow leopard's four paws hit the hard ground.

Poised on the wall she had momentarily forgotten the paw she had injured when hunting the wild blue sheep, but when she hit the rocky floor of the compound an agonizing shock of pain went through her whole body. She screeched, and the pain was so intense that for five or six seconds she was unable to move.

In those few seconds the sheep and goats came to frightened life. Baaing and bleating, they tried vainly to hide behind one another. The dogs were still snarling over the hot mutton, but Shainu and Temba quickly scrambled to their feet.

In the flickering light of the fire there was a moment when only the terrified sheep and goats were moving, bunching in one corner as far as possible from the danger. The snow leopard, her lips drawn back in a snarl of pain, faced the two humans. She was the first to move. Ignoring the pain, and somehow managing a three-legged leap, she reached the flock and made her kill. One blow was sufficient. It was a quick, clean death; the victim never knew what happened.

With the sheep in her jaws she turned, but now the dogs had got her scent. The nearest, a two-year-old mastiff with more courage than fighting skill, rushed in recklessly, his eyes green-lit with ferocity. He died as quickly as the sheep had died as one sweeping hammer blow from the snow leopard's uninjured paw took him on the side of the head, hurling him a yard away, his neck broken.

By this time Shainu had cocked his rifle and pushed the safety catch to the "off" position. Roaring to the remaining dogs to stand clear, he took quick aim. Temba had hurriedly grabbed a three-foot length of bamboo. Several of these sticks were always kept by the fireside for emergencies since bamboo, with its hard shiny skin that kept out the rain and its oily wood inside, caught fire quickly and was ideal for torches.

As Temba poked his torch deeper into the fire there was a thunderous roar from his father's rifle. Shainu could not afford to buy the expensive .303 cartridges that burned cordite. Instead, he used ammunition bought from a village gunsmith, refilling used cartridge cases with cheap black gunpowder. Some misfired, but those that did fire produced an explosion that sounded like a small cannon. Shainu Droma liked the big bang, for often enough it would scare away an enemy, even if the bullet did not find its target.

In the past he had been very successful in his shooting, but this time he was unlucky. As he fired, another dog sprang at the snow leopard, and the bullet that should have killed the snow leopard hit the mastiff between the shoulders, killing him instantly. Shar, the last of the dogs, was looking anxiously at Shainu, waiting for a command, but there was no time for commands. Startled and angered, the snow leopard sprang at the hillman.

"Look out!" Temba screamed. He swung the burning bamboo in an effort to scare off the attacker, but he was far too slow. Shainu, in any case, needed no warning from his son. He was leaping away even as the snow leopard sprang at him. For a big man Shainu was quick, but this time he was not quick enough. A right paw struck him on the shoulder and hurled him backward. As he hit the ground Shainu began to roll. He expected to be pounced on; instead, the leopard made for the partly broken-down wall where she had first entered the compound. She was speeded in her retreat by Temba swinging his bamboo torch and shrieking.

Everything had happened quickly. Little more than a minute had passed since the snow leopard had first leaped into the compound. Forced to drop the dead sheep when the first mastiff had attacked her, she now had to leave without her prize. In the flickering light of the fire she looked like a blur of pale, spotted gold as, belly to the ground, she limped across to the wall and, hampered by the damaged forepaw, somehow managed to heave herself up.

Though knocked down by the snow leopard, Shainu had not dropped his rifle. Rolling over twice he bounced to his feet like a circus acrobat. Expertly he jerked back the rifle bolt, ejected the spent cartridge, and rammed a new round of ammunition into the smoking breech. It was done quickly, but the snow leopard was already leaping off the wall when he fired. The muzzle spat flame a yard long, and above the thunder of the shot came a scream of triumph from Temba. The spotted form had seemed to roll sideways as it disappeared from sight.

"You hit her! You hit her!"

"The torch!" his father yelled, hurriedly reloading. He snatched the flaming bamboo, yelled a command to the last of his three dogs and ran across to the wall. Holding his torch high, he peered over. He, too, was sure he had hit her, yet the snow leopard was not there. Hurriedly he scrambled over the wall, and Shar, his dog, went ahead. Shainu Droma's eyes were blazing with excitement. He had lost two dogs and a sheep, but if he got this snow leopard then the night could still be profitable, for the skin of a snow leopard would always bring a good price in the market at Rakfazar Bazaar. Hot with the excitement of the hunter, Shainu raced after his mastiff.

This was not the first time their camp had been attacked, and the Droma family had its own plan of action for such occasions. Had his mother and sister been in the camp, Temba would have followed his father with another torch while they would have lighted other torches and stayed behind to defend the flock. Since his mother and sister were not there, Temba's duty was to stay in the compound, leaving it only if his father shouted for assistance.

"Come on, come on," he grumbled as another bamboo he had thrust into the fire seemed slow in starting to burn. "Hurry . . . hurry . . . hurry!"

A minute later he heard his father's rifle roar for the third time, and at the sound a grin of triumph lighted Temba's face. That would be the finish. His father had been unlucky with his first shot, but the second bullet had not missed. He had seen the pale gold body of the snow leopard jerk, which meant that she was hit.

Waving his torch gently from side to side until the end

was burning furiously, Temba hurried to the partly broken wall and peered over, expecting to see his father's torch thirty or forty yards away. He was puzzled when he could see nothing—neither torch nor man nor dog.

The quarter moon had lifted itself clear of the mountain peaks and was shedding a pale white light over the scene. It shimmered on patches of snow, deceiving the eyes. Temba called his father by name but there was no answer. Suddenly frightened, he scrambled over the wall. As he did so, he thought he saw a tiny, flickering light, sixty or more yards away. It was no more than a spot of red, and Temba moved toward it, shouting and waving his own torch. He knew the danger from a wounded snow leopard, and as he ran he drew the long knife he carried at his waist belt. It was a two-handed weapon, with a sixteen-inch blade. With it a man could slash through bamboo or timber—and it was a deadly weapon in a fight.

"Coming, Father. COMING!" Though he yelled as loudly as he could, there was no reply. When he was a dozen yards from the guttering torch, he realized it was lying on the ground. Temba stopped. His heart was thumping, and a strange, terrible fear made him feel cold inside. What had happened? Why did his father not reply? He had fired his rifle and, because even black-powder cartridges were expensive, Shainu Droma seldom fired until he was sure of hitting his target.

Had he stumbled and shot himself? At the thought Temba's heart gave a convulsive leap. Such things did sometimes happen, and in this moonlight, hurrying over uneven ground, any man could stumble. Slowly, always holding his knife ready, Temba approached the flickering torch. Burned down to a six-inch stub, it lay on the edge of a small patch of snow. His father had been here; and since he must have been in this place, the dog should also have been here. The dog had never been known to desert his master. Where had they gone? Temba's brain seemed frozen. Nothing like this had ever happened to him before. No father, no dog, no snow leopard—even though the rifle had been fired. The rifle! Where was it? He looked around and saw no sign of that, either. Then, to add to his fear, the sputtering torch on the ground went out. It was like a sign to Temba; it, too, had died!

2
Night
of Disaster

TEMBA HAD BEEN RIGHT WHEN HE YELLED TRIUM-
phantly that the snow leopard had been hit. The bullet
had cut a faint crease in the fur on top of her skull. It
scarcely drew blood, but the impact had been like a blow
from a club. It had dazed her, and she had rolled heavily
off the wall. But instinct and fear had brought her to
her feet and sent her in a staggering run for the edge
of the cliff. Her lair was at its foot, but she was still too
dazed to realize where she was going or that she had
reached the edge of the cliff at the wrong place. At this
point there was no path. Had she gone over here she
would have plunged sixty feet to the river below. Still
dazed, the snow leopard stood staring down at the river,
which in the light of the moon looked like a silver sheet.
As the mists began to clear from her head, the snow leopard turned aside, and as she did so, Shainu Droma's
mastiff, Shar, came racing up.

Had the hillman not arrived behind him the night
would have ended very differently. Shar would have

attacked, and either he or the snow leopard would have died within the minute. They were both fighters—both fierce, both brave; there would have been no drawing back. Shainu knew this and roared at his dog to stand clear.

Snarling ferociously, his emerald eyes piercing in the moonlight, Shar obeyed. He moved to one side, blocking the one way the snow leopard could retreat. Now that her head had cleared, she was desperately anxious to get to the path and back to her lair and her kittens at the foot of the cliff. Suddenly screeching her fury at the dog that barred her way, she turned and leaped.

As she moved, Shainu Droma fired. It was his third shot of the evening—and his third miss. Before he could reload the snow leopard was on him. Shainu had just time enough to lift his rifle to keep her fangs from his throat, before he was borne backward under her weight.

Shar needed no urging to come to his master's defense. With a low whimper he hurled himself at the struggling pair. Shainu Droma, already off balance, was staggering in his effort to keep the snow leopard's fangs from his throat. The dog's weight, as he sprang onto the snow leopard's back, was more than even a strong hillman could withstand. He reeled, unable to keep his balance —and backed over the edge of the cliff.

For one frightening moment the three bodies were outlined against the moonlit valley—man, snow leopard, and dog. Strangely enough, not one of them cried out. Soundlessly they plummeted through sixty feet of space toward the ice cold river gurgling below.

As they fell, they separated. Shainu Droma dropped

his rifle. With the inborn agility of the cat tribe the snow leopard hurled herself away from the hillman, twisted, and, falling head first, hit the water. There were three splashes, all within the space of a split second. Three spouts of silver-bright water were thrown high, to sparkle brilliantly in the moonlight. Then the river surface smoothed itself out again. The three black forms were gone, with nothing to show they had fallen.

There was quiet for several minutes. Then from the top of the cliff came a frantic voice: "Father! *Father!* F A T H E R!"

A few seconds later Temba's shouts were answered as the hills across the valley threw back his voice in a ghostly echo: "Father! Father! F A T H E R!" The echoes were repeated several times, growing fainter and fainter until they were swallowed up by the night.

Temba knew all about echoes, for like all hill people, he believed they came from evil spirits mocking the mere human being. The disappearance of his father, the dog, the rifle, and the snow leopard were terrifying enough; now, to have an evil spirit mocking him was more than Temba could bear.

Turning, he raced back to the compound as if *shaitan* (Satan) himself were at his heels. By the time he reached the camp his eyes were bulging with terror, for he was sure an evil spirit was chasing him. Not daring to slow down to scramble over the wall, he made a magnificent leap that carried him over the top and landed him within a yard of the dying fire.

There was an uneasy shuffling from the sheep and goats. Heads turned in his direction and eyes showed purple in the ruddy glow. Temba was too frightened even to speak to the animals. Hastily spreading firewood over the red embers, he fanned the fire vigorously with his fur cap. As he fanned, he watched the wall, afraid that at any moment one of the dreaded spirits of the hills would leap over and come for him.

His face, burned brick red by the harsh mountain winds and the reflected light of the summer sun on the snows, had lost some of its color. Had his father been with him, it would all have been different. Temba was no coward. Dangers from wild animals, from winter storms, even from spring avalanches, were all part of the hill boy's life. Throughout his thirteen years he had lived side by side with sudden death; it was the unknown that frightened him: the strange disappearance of his father and the dog, *and* the voice calling to him from across the valley.

Evil spirits! The two words hammered loudly in his brain. Evil spirits! He knew that a boy like himself was powerless against evil spirits. Even his father and mother were afraid of them. Yet as minute followed minute and nothing happened, gradually the wild racing of his heart slowed down. The sheep and goats were settling to sleep again, which was usually a good sign. Temba knew that if there was danger, they would sense it before a human being.

It was the heat of the fire that helped him most. As the new firewood began to burn and give off a reassuring crackle, the kettle started to hiss and splutter and the mutton soup bubbled and plopped. The appetizing smell of the mutton reminded Temba that he had eaten nothing

since the previous evening save for their meager breakfast. He bent and dipped a finger into the mutton stew
and whistled at the scalding heat as he flicked the hot
soup off his finger.

Casting a last anxious look around the firelit walls,
he knelt down. He was ravenously hungry. "If evil spirits
come or if the snow leopard comes," he asked himself,
"what can Temba Droma do, since he has no gun? Is
a knife good against evil spirits?" He drew his long heavy
blade from its sheath, looked at it, and ran a thumb
lightly along the edge. Razor keen! The hill people
tested the sharpness of their knives on wool plucked from
the back of a sheep. If the blade cut through wool
cleanly, then the knife was sharp enough.

Feeling a bit more confident, Temba laid his knife
where he could grab it in an instant and dipped his
father's mug into the mutton pot. But the mutton was
too hot even for his taste, so he filled his own mug with
tea, waited for it to cool, then gulped down a mouthful
before taking a chunk of the dripping mutton.

He ate quickly at first, but by the time his appetite was
beginning to be satisfied he was eating slowly and really
enjoying the food. The mutton had simmered longer
than usual at the edge of the fire, so it was well cooked,
while the soup was thick and nourishing. He finished the
meal with another mug of tea and sat wiping the greasy
blade of his knife when he heard a sound that brought
back all his fears. Yet, strangely enough, it brought a
suggestion of hope, too.

The night wind was sighing plaintively up the valley,
but this was not what caused the new sound. Temba

recognized it at once; it was the far-off howl of a dog! Temba was on his feet in an instant, his knife half raised. One or two of the flock lifted their heads, then closed their eyes again when nothing more happened.

Anxiously Temba listened. From puppy days their dogs were taught by kicks and cuffs to keep silent. They were only allowed to bark when a stranger was approaching, or when he and his father were trying to pen a bear or some other four-legged marauder. As he listened, Temba tried not to believe the first thought that came to his mind—that the howl was that of a spirit dog. No, he recognized the howling; it was their dog, the old one, Shar, their best guard dog. He was sure it was Shar.

The night seemed suddenly very quiet. Temba could hear the faint *plop-plop-plop* of the mutton soup in the pot as it simmered gently. A sheep sneezed. The sound was like an explosion and caused Temba to swing around, muscles tense, knife raised. Then the howling came again. It was thin and faraway, yet there was no mistaking it. It *was* Shar. Temba grabbed one of the bamboo fire sticks and thrust the end into the heart of the fire.

"That *is* Shar," he muttered. "I would know his bark anywhere. My father must be with him. They went out together. They will be together now. The dog would not leave him."

He was afraid, but driven on by hope he scrambled over the wall. He did not need the torch to show him the way, for the quarter moon was brilliant now, and the mountain peaks were silver in its light.

Temba made for the spot where he had found his

father's guttering torch and picked up the charred frag-
ment of bamboo. He looked from it to the edge of the
cliff, four yards distant, and wondered if his father might
have fallen over the cliff. Then he shrugged and almost
laughed at such a stupid idea. "Shainu Droma is surefooted as a goat," he scoffed, yet he still wondered un-
easily *if* he might have fallen.

Striding to the very edge he looked down the sixty-
foot drop. The river ran silver in the moonlight, its
glistening path broken here and there by rocks showing
as dark patches. He could see the skeleton outlines of
shrubs that had been washed down by the previous
spring floods. They were long dead. Everything was
dead. Nothing moved. It was a valley of frightening
silence.

Then the dog howled again.

The sound was clearer now, and there was no doubt
it came from somewhere down by the water. Temba
cupped his hands about his mouth and called the dog by
name: "Shar! *Shar!* SHAR!" There was an echo some
ten seconds later from across the valley; but this time
the echo did not frighten him, for Temba already had
an answer. Not the bark he had expected, but an answer that made his heart bound with joy and hope. From
the bottom of the cliff, where the river ran so smoothly
in the moonlight, came the faint cry of a man. Shainu
Droma was alive!

"I come, Father, I come!" Temba yelled, waving his
torch. He turned to look for the path that he knew led
down the face of the cliff, but was halted almost at once

by a warning cry from his father: "Temba! TEMBA! Remember the snow leopard. She may be near. Have your knife ready. Make sure your torch will last for some time."

Temba hated the delay, but he hurried back to the compound and armed himself with three extra pieces of bamboo. Then he rushed back to the cliff. He went down to the river level, sliding much of the way in his anxiety to reach his father.

Shainu Droma was on the opposite side of the water. To reach him, Temba had to wade through the icy cold current, which at this point was almost waist deep in the middle. But he crossed safely and soon found his father lying on the bank. Propping his torch against a boulder Temba said, "I thought the hill demons had taken you. I stood up there earlier and called, but there was no reply."

"I heard you," his father said gruffly, then added, "But when a man has fallen a great distance, and has had to fight for his life in the river, he needs time before he can answer his son."

"Are you badly hurt?" Temba asked, knowing that his father would not be lying so still if he was not hurt.

"I am hurt," his father agreed, "but how badly I do not know. That *shaitan* got her claws into my leg, and I have bled."

"I will get you on my back," Temba said anxiously, "and then I——" but his father cut him short.

"Find the dog. He is near, and he is the only dog we have now. He is farther downstream. Have a care with him. If he is badly injured he will snap at you. If he is dying——"

"Dying!" Temba did not often interrupt his father, but the thought that their one remaining dog might be dying appalled him.

"He fell, as I fell." Shainu Droma was impatient. Not only was he in pain, but the cold was biting through his sodden clothes like a knife. "I fell and hit the water where it was deep. The dog may have been less lucky. If his legs are broken, put him out of his misery. One does not leave a dog to die in pain."

"Yes, Father." Reluctantly Temba went off to look for Shar, holding his torch high, even though it was bright moonlight. He called their old dog and was answered at once. Shar was lying half in, half out of the water, jammed by the current into the branches of a dead bush. Temba's heart sank as he hacked at the branches with his heavy knife. The dog must surely be badly hurt or he would have freed himself long ago. Even when he released the mastiff, Shar lay still, staring at his young master, his green eyes flickering in the moonlight.

Carefully Temba checked each of the mastiff's legs. They did not seem to be broken, yet Shar made no attempt to get to his feet. Temba pondered whether he should kill him or let him live. In the high hills dogs are not pets; they earn their food by guarding their flocks and by guarding the family. When a dog can no longer do that he must find his own food.

As if he knew what was passing through Temba's mind, the old mastiff suddenly made a great effort and heaved himself shakily to his feet.

"Come," Temba ordered, starting to walk back to his father. The mastiff tried to obey, but fell. Bravely he struggled to his feet again, managed two steps, then fell once more.

Temba sheathed his knife. Kneeling down he lifted the dog across his shoulders. Shar was heavy, but no heavier than some of the burdens Temba had carried.

"I think he will live," he told his father. "Shall I light a torch for you?"

"Your knife will be better. That snow leopard is starving. Return quickly."

Shainu did not say that he was half frozen, but Temba knew how his father must feel, for his own clothes were clinging to him in an icy grip. After lighting a new bamboo, he picked up the mastiff again and his own half-burned torch and began to recross the stream. Halfway over he slipped, and while regaining his balance, dropped the torch. It hit the water and died. But the moon gave ample light. As he reached the foot of the cliffs, he laid the dog down for a moment. Suddenly, the snow leopard stood before him, barring the way.

Temba had passed the mouth of her lair earlier, but then his eyes had been on the river. At the snow leopard's warning snarl, he straightened and looked into the living green fire of her eyes. Only when his hand fumbled over the top of his empty scabbard did Temba remember that he had left his long knife with his father. As if his fear had been passed on to the dog at his feet, the mastiff gave a growl of defiance. Shakily Shar rose, the coarse hair on his neck stiff with anger.

The snow leopard, her pale gold body blending with

her background, shrank down, her eyes blazing. From her throat came a warning, like the clacking of a wooden cogwheel, and her tail twitched nervously—a sign that she was about to spring.

Without knife or torch Temba stood rigid. He knew that the first move he made would be like squeezing the trigger of a gun. The snow leopard's spring-taut muscles would catapult her onto him, and her deadly claws would rip through clothing and flesh like razor-sharp daggers. Yet, whether he moved or not, she was going to leap. Her eyes had closed to the narrowest of slits. Temba's muscles were taut. He dared not take his eyes off her. There was nothing he could do to help the dog at his feet. He had to decide which way to leap.

For seconds that seemed hours, Temba and his crippled dog stared at the crouching snow leopard. The green eyes sank a little nearer to the ground. Now for the leap!

At that second, from somewhere within the darkness of the cave came a pathetic little *meow, meow*! A snow-leopard kitten was crying for more milk.

There was a momentary flurry of movement. Then the blazing green eyes vanished and Temba and his mastiff were alone. Knowing her kitten needed her, the snow leopard had retreated into the darkness.

3
A Battle
for Life

WEAK AND SHAKEN WITH FRIGHT, TEMBA PICKED UP Shar and carried him to the top of the cliff. Some strength seemed to be returning to the mastiff's shaky legs, but not enough to carry him to the compound. After a short rest, Temba struggled across the little plateau and laid Shar near the fire.

When he went back to the river he carried a mug of mutton with him, and his father grunted his surprise and satisfaction. The soup was little more than lukewarm, yet it was welcome. When he had finished eating, Temba helped his father across the swollen stream and up the cliff. By this time the last of Temba's bamboo torches was burning out. Fortunately, they saw no sign of the snow leopard.

The fire, which had been burning so brightly in the compound, was now no more than a handful of warm gray ashes. Like his father, Temba was exhausted, but he split kindlings, then coaxed a spot of red fire to life and built it up until the flames were leaping high.

Soon more soup was bubbling in the pot and Shainu Droma's sodden clothes were steaming in the heat. Father and son sat close to the blaze, for neither had a change of clothing. When they had eaten more mutton, Temba opened one of the packs and brought out some home-cured tobacco. As Shainu smoked, he stretched out his right leg and stroked it gently. Only then did Temba notice that the rough material was slashed to ribbons. Shainu gave a disgusted grunt. "*Tcha!*" he said. "I tell you this, son of mine, never again shall I boast that I am a mighty hunter. This night I was a fool, and I paid dearly for my foolishness. The dog had cornered the spotted hunter on the cliff top, and was ready to go in and finish her off. Remembering he was our only dog, I called him off. I was so sure the leopard was badly wounded, and so sure that I could finish her with my gun." He spat into the fire and sat staring in silence for a moment. Then he went on. "Round many a campfire I have heard men say how terrible a wounded leopard is when cornered. Now I know those tellers of tales were speaking the truth. As the dog turned aside, the leopard leaped. I fired, and missed. Yes, for the third time in a single night I missed. I did not get another chance. The spotted *shaitan* was on me, and my leg will carry the scars to the day I die."

He dug a sliver of bamboo into the edge of the fire and with it relit his pipe. After puffing for a moment or so he went on in the same disgusted voice. "Three shots in one night, and all I have done is kill my youngest dog. Then the old one almost killed me. When the leopard was clawing me, the dog leaped onto her, and so we all went over the cliff."

"A good spirit must have been with you," Temba said. "It is a long way to fall and live."

His father nodded. "I thought I would die," he admitted. "I remember seeing the river as I fell. It looked like a bar of silver. The next thing I knew, I was half out of the water and you were calling me . . . and I could not answer."

He sat smoking until the tobacco was dead ash. Temba dozed. He had noticed with alarm the badly slashed trouser leg and the gashes at the shoulder and the throat of the quilted coat. He realized that if the snow leopard had not been hampered by a damaged forepaw not even the quilted coat would have saved his father; the dagger claws would have got through to the flesh below. Although Shainu's clothes were torn, Temba thought his father had escaped injury since he had not complained, but a command to cut away the torn trouser leg awakened him from his doze. "And be careful," Shainu ordered. "That spotted devil has ripped me to pieces. The pain is like a drumbeat going up my leg—*thrum-thrum-thrum.*"

Temba shot a quick glance at his father. He had never heard him speak like this before. Accidents happened in the high hills, and pain was something the hill people learned to bear without complaint; even women did not cry out at pain. In the clean, rarefied air, wounds healed quickly. Yet there was a strange note in Shainu Droma's voice, and there was a dew of sweat on his forehead.

When Temba cut away the slashed trouser leg his eyes widened at the sight of the savage wounds. The snow leopard's claws had gashed the hillman's leg from just below the knee down to the ankle. Temba did not know what to do. His mother had a bag in which she kept dried plants from the Indian plains. The plants, named *Brahm Buti* (God's flower), were soaked in water, then the water from the stems was squeezed out into the wound. After such doctoring wounds often healed in a day or so. But Temba's mother was not with them, and her bag of dried plants had not been brought along.

"Fetch water from the river," Shainu said quietly.

"From the river?" Temba was astonished. "But there is snow here in the compound. I could melt———"

"It must be water from the river," his father insisted, and his face was now twisted in a frown of pain. "Once I met a white man in the hills who had been clawed by a bear. White men are clever, and he swore that water from old snow did not help a wound to heal. He also said hot water must be used to clean a wound. So we will have it so hot that I may cry out when it is poured into these wounds. Pain will not matter if the wound heals quickly."

"Pour hot water into the claw wounds!" Temba was horrified at the idea.

"It is the only way," Shainu insisted. "I knew a man who was clawed by a leopard. He was a strong man, as I am a strong man; yet he died within a week."

"Died!" Temba's eyes bulged. The thought of his father dying made his heart thump painfully. Surely his father could not die! If Shainu Droma died Temba's world would come to an end. His father's voice brought him back to earth.

Wiping the beads of sweat from his forehead, Shainu said, "Since that day I have heard strange things about leopards. It is said that a scratch from a leopard's claws brings a strange evil spirit into the blood, and it can only be washed out with water hot enough to make tea."

"But water from the river!"

"Yes, *water from the river*," his father insisted. "Those who know these things say river water is best for washing the evil spirit away."

"I go for water," Temba said. He picked up the teakettle, lit a torch, and made sure his knife was loose in its scabbard. The snow leopard might be prowling at the foot of the cliff. It was a frightening thought and it reminded him of their missing rifle.

"The rifle!" Shainu said when Temba mentioned it. "That must wait until tomorrow. It must be in the river —and you will seek it. Without a rifle what can even I do in these hills? Now fetch the water."

Temba took less than twenty minutes to get to the river, fill his kettle, and bring it back to the compound. He did not see the snow leopard. He pushed the kettle into the glowing embers at the fringe of the fire and waited anxiously. They had arrived at this spot as the sun was setting and in the five hours that had passed Temba's world had been turned topsy-turvy. Now, as the teakettle neared boiling, he became more and more worried.

When steam made the kettle lid begin to dance, Temba

looked anxiously at his father. "Father," he murmured, "do you remember the time last year when we were at Rakfazar Bazaar and my sister upset a kettle of hot water over her feet? There were blisters."

"I remember," his father agreed.

"And you want me to pour this water, which is hot enough to make tea, into the wounds? There will be blisters, and——"

"There will not be blisters," Shainu interrupted angrily. "For some reason I do not understand, water will boil in the high hills and yet not be as hot as water that boils in the valley. Take the kettle from the fire and with the water clean these wounds before the poison devil kills me."

Temba took the kettle, and a few seconds later Shainu Droma roared in agony. Temba drew back, fearful of what his father would do, but after a few moments he was ordered to finish the job. Shainu Droma was tough, and he had expected pain, but as more steaming water splashed into the claw wounds he could not hold back the howls of anguish. Yet, because Shainu Droma had seen a man die from blood poisoning, he ordered Temba to empty every drop of hot water into the gashes.

After he had wiped the sweat of agony from his face, Shainu refilled his pipe. He asked Temba to wrap the lacerated leg in a piece of old rag, and when the bandaging was finished, he told his son that he could sleep.

The hill boy was glad to lie down. Believing his father knew everything, he no longer worried about the claw wounds. The hot water would have driven the devil from the wounds, and his father would recover. He was quite sure that within a day or two they would be on their way down the pass to Rakfazar Bazaar.

Temba woke with the dawn. After he had drunk a mug of tea his father ordered him to go down to the river to search for the lost rifle. After looking from the top of the cliff at the spot where his father had fallen over, he went warily down to the river. A rifle would not float, so there should be little difficulty in finding the weapon.

There was no sign of the snow leopard at the water's edge, and for the first time since reaching the plateau Temba was lucky. He had expected that he would have to wade into the stream to find the rifle, but when the rifle fell it had plunged through the yard-deep water, struck a stone, and snapped the butt away from the barrel. The butt had floated, but because it was connected to the barrel by a carrying strap, the current had not been able to bear it downstream. It was the floating butt that caught Temba's eye and helped him retrieve the weapon without even having to wade into the water.

When he dragged it ashore, however, his heart sank, for the weapon seemed to be smashed beyond repair. Sadly he carried it back to his father. At that moment the tragedy of the broken Lee-Enfield rifle seemed more serious than Shainu's leg wounds.

His father took the two parts and stared at them for a long time, then tried to fit them together. "An hour's careful work by a gunsmith would see the rifle as good as new," he said, but Shainu was no gunsmith. "Dry the parts and grease them," he told his son. Then, to Temba's surprise, he lay down with his face toward the ground.

"Do we stay here today?" Temba asked, not realizing

that his father was lying face down so that his son would not see the agony in his eyes. After a few moments Temba repeated his question.

"Graze the sheep and goats," Shainu said in a queer, jerky voice. "We stay."

Temba was puzzled, but since no hill boy ever questioned a command from his father, he carefully dried the smashed rifle, wiped every part with butter, and even contrived to draw a greased rag through the barrel as he had seen his father do. When he wrapped the broken parts in rags, his face showed the sorrow he felt. His father had bought the onetime British army rifle four years ago, and had promised his son that one day the weapon would be his. Now it was broken.

The sheep and goats were nibbling at a pile of snow. They had not had a chance to drink since the previous morning when Shainu and Temba had broken the ice on a pool in the pass. The sheep killed by the snow leopard lay where it had fallen, as did the two dogs.

Sadly Temba carried the bodies of the dogs one by one to the nearest cliff edge and dropped them over. The dead sheep, which he would skin and cut up later on, would provide them with food for two or three days. As for the flock, he did not know quite what to do. They were clamoring for food, and his father had said to take them out to graze. Temba wondered if his father had forgotten the snow leopard. He was almost about to wake him to ask for advice, but then decided against this. When Shainu Droma said to do something, he meant it to be done.

Going to the part of the wall where stones had fallen from the top, Temba looked toward the north. Far up on the hillside he could make out a collection of tiny dots, a flock of the wild mountain sheep. Perhaps the snow leopard would be stalking them. Temba hoped so when he let their baaing, bleating flock out. They were all anxious to get at the sweet new grass now poking its way through the thin layer of snow. Throughout the winter their food had been the upland hay, and the animals were pining for grass.

He dragged aside the bundles of thorny scrub that blocked the entrance to the compound, and with eager baaing and bleating the sheep and goats trotted out. Now the dogs would have been useful. They would not only have kept the flock from scattering, but they would have made any snow leopard cautious about approaching.

Temba had examined Shar and had given him a meal of raw mutton. The dog was badly bruised and so stiff he could hardly limp about, but he did not appear to have any broken bones. Temba was hopeful that after a day or so he would be fit again. For the present, he was of no use for herding, and Temba did not attempt to take him outside the compound.

Heads down, the sheep and goats began to graze, cropping swiftly. Soon they were spreading out, and Temba spent the next twenty minutes acting as herd dog, trying to keep them fairly close together.

Then, without warning, the snow leopard appeared.

Crouched down at the top of the cliff, she studied the flock, nineteen sheep and sixteen goats. Temba was circling them, trying hard to keep them in a compact group that he could control. It was the morning wind, now blowing off the mountain and down to the distant plains, that carried the snow leopard's scent to the grazers.

Heads, which had been bent to the thin grass, were lifted and thirty-five pairs of eyes turned to stare in the direction of the snow leopard. The sudden alertness of his flock warned Temba of danger. He could see nothing alarming. There had been no sound, but with a frightened bleat the nearest sheep suddenly sped toward the hill boy. There was an immediate rush by the others, and in less than a minute Temba was besieged by a bleating, baaing crowd of frightened animals. Those on the outside were even leaping onto the backs of their companions in an effort to get nearer the hill boy.

The snow leopard raised herself from her crouching position, stared, then snarled. Now Temba saw her. He drew his big knife, waved it in the morning sun, and yelled angrily. The spotted hunter pulled back a few paces. Men were the one thing she did not understand. Their smell was strange and the sounds they made were frightening. Now, however, hunger conquered fear. As Temba began his retreat toward the stone-walled compound, with the sheep and goats in a noisy rabble around him, the snow leopard limped after them.

Temba increased his speed, walking backward so that he could watch the snow leopard. Had she not been hampered by her damaged forepaw, the snow leopard certainly would have rushed the clamoring mob of sheep and goats. That would have panicked them into scattering, making a kill easy. As it was, she could limp only a little more quickly than Temba and his frightened flock could move.

Twice he halted her advance by breaking clear of the ring of frightened animals and rushing forward, waving his long knife and screaming abuse. Each time his shouts and the flash of sunlight on the knife blade drove the snow leopard back a little.

An old billy goat helped win the battle. When they were about twenty yards from the compound, the veteran suddenly butted one of his wives and within seconds he had the frightened mob streaking toward the entrance. Temba raced with them and dragged the bundles of thorny twigs across the opening just in time to force the snarling snow leopard to slither to a halt.

She stood there, glaring at him, a queer clacking sound coming from deep in her throat. Finally she limped to one side, and Temba lost sight of her behind the wall.

Five minutes later the leopard reappeared. Hunger had given her the courage to climb onto the lowest part of the wall, and she poised there, the sun gleaming on her pale gold hide. Her tail streamed out behind her, helping to balance her on the top of the wall. Her teeth were bared in a soundless, menacing snarl, and only the fear of hurting her already damaged forepaw kept her from springing down to make a kill among the terrified sheep and goats.

The increased clamor warned Temba, who had been looking at his father, that there was danger, and swinging around, he faced the intruder.

Grabbing his big knife, he looked desperately for some better weapon. What he could do with a knife against a starving snow leopard, he did not know. Suddenly paralyzed by fear, he could only stand and stare.

The snow leopard broke the paralysis. She slithered part way down the wall, snarling as her injured paw touched a stone and sent a shock wave of pain to her shoulder.

Now Temba came to life. Stooping, he grabbed a flaming stick from the fire and threw it. It sped through the air, scattering sparks. The snow leopard drew back, snarling. But this time she was not going to retreat. Then Temba threw something else—a large piece of mutton. It landed almost at the snow leopard's feet and she snatched it up. Once again Temba yelled and waved his knife.

Within seconds the danger was over. With the mutton in her jaws, the snow leopard scrambled up the wall, paused for a second on the top, then dropped to the other side.

4
"She Will Come Again"

THE CLAMOR OF THE SHEEP AND GOATS PENETRATED the mists gathering about Shainu Droma. While his son had been out with the flock he had tried to stand, but the pain in his foot and leg had wrung from him a groan of agony. Like all hillmen Shainu had known many kinds of pain in his life. And, like all those who lived a wandering life in the mountainous countries of Bhutan, Sikkim, and Nepal, he hardly knew what the word *doctor* meant. For sickness or injuries the hill people used their own simple remedies; when those did not work, they died.

Shainu called Temba to him and told him to take the rag off the wound. He said nothing of the increasing pain, but he watched his son's face when the not-very-clean bandage was taken off and he saw the boy's expression change. The fear and bewilderment in Temba's eyes made Shainu heave himself into a sitting position to look at the wounds.

The deep slashes gave every sign of infection. A dull

purple path led from the wounds up the leg. It was an unmistakable sign of blood poisoning, but Shainu had never seen anything like it before.

"What is happening?" Temba asked, deep concern in his voice. "Is this because I poured hot water on your leg?"

Shainu lay back. For the first time in his life he thought he was going to die. He was not afraid of death, but he was afraid of what would happen to his son. What could a young boy do alone in these hills? To make matters worse, he was without a rifle, and his only help was a sick dog. He would never be able to manage the flock of sheep and goats. Then another thought occurred to Shainu. He remembered his wife and daughter waiting for them back in the hills. His wife was unable to walk. True, they were not desperately short of food, for Shainu had left at least half of his sheep and goats with them; but if Temba could not get back with supplies purchased at Rakfazar Bazaar, death would come to them when winter closed in again.

Shainu tried not to show the fear that was bringing beads of sweat onto his face.

"My son," he said, "I shall not be able to walk for some days. Yet if we stay here that accursed *shaitan* that attacked us last night will come again——"

"I have just given her part of a sheep," Temba interrupted.

"She will come again," his father insisted. "I saw last night that she was limping. If she cannot get food by hunting the usual way she will come here again and again—a sheep tomorrow, a goat the day after. When she realizes we have neither a gun nor dogs, she will grow even bolder."

"I will make a spear," Temba said eagerly. "Perhaps I could dig a pit and trap her."

Shainu shook his head wearily.

"Only a boy would say a thing like that. My son, this ground is too hard to dig. Not only is the coldness of winter still in it, but there are rocks beneath the thin soil. You could not dig a pit. As for a spear—that would be useless against a snow leopard. They are as quick as the lightning that leaps from sky to earth. And since she is a mother with young, that makes the danger even worse."

Temba squatted on his heels and waited. He knew his father must have decided what was to be done, and a thirteen-year-old boy did not ask too many questions.

Shainu lay with closed eyes for several minutes. He was not finding it easy to concentrate, for the blood poisoning was already having its effect. There was a growing fever in his blood, and he found it difficult to think clearly.

At last he forced himself to a sitting position and spoke. "Gather enough firewood to last three days. Open the bales of hay. Put them near me so that I can keep the sheep and goats from eating too much at one time. I shall need water, for there is a fire in my blood that makes me thirsty. Gather some snow and put that near me to satisfy my thirst while you are away."

Temba was startled. "While I am away?" he asked.

"Where am I going, Father? Is it not better for me to stay here and guard you and our flock?"

"You will go down to Rakfazar Bazaar," his father said. "Take enough sheep and goats to carry sufficient goods to pay for the mending of the rifle and the purchase of a pony. Without a rifle we cannot kill this spotted hunter, and without a pony I shall not live. But you must not sell a sheep or a goat."

Temba's eyes bulged. The very thought that his father might die filled him with a terrible fear. Shainu Droma stood for everything that was strong and wise. He guarded the family against wild beasts. He knew how to handle the occasional homeless men who wandered the hills in search of weak, defenseless travelers. Shainu Droma was everything: father, guardian, hunter, adviser. Temba could not imagine how they could live without him.

As if guessing what was going through his son's mind, Shainu forced a smile. He laid a reassuring hand on Temba's shoulder.

"I shall not die, my son, for you will get a pony down in the Bazaar. Though this accursed snow leopard has slashed me and left a burning devil in my leg, it can be driven out. For the past three years a *memsahib* has come to Rakfazar Bazaar. She is a strange woman. Who but a white *memsahib* would travel without a husband to protect her? Yet in other ways she has great wisdom. I have watched her make the sick better. I have seen knife wounds that she has healed—terrible knife wounds. I know she can heal this wound of mine."

While he closed his eyes and wearily wiped the sweat of pain from his forehead, Temba stared past him and said nothing. He had traveled the high passes from Bhutan to the village known as Rakfazar Bazaar once each year ever since he could remember. As a baby he had traveled straddling his mother's hip, and those days had been the easiest for him. Once he could walk he had had to hang on to the tail of an older sheep as they climbed the stony tracks into the cloud-covered upper passes. Up there, where neither eagle nor raven flew, where there was no grass or trees and the whistling wind cut to the bone, life was hard even for the hill people. The wind was often full of driving snow, or hail, which stung the cheeks like leaden shot. The flocks fed on a daily handful of hay, and a frozen pool would be smashed open so that they could drink.

Temba had known that kind of thing all his life and was not afraid of it. What he did fear was going to Rakfazar Bazaar alone.

The downhill journey would not worry him. Before the end of a day's march there would be lush grass and babbling streams, which had lost their icy coldness. It was when they reached the little village, with its once-a-year market, that his difficulties would begin.

Their packs containing precious *lac*, yaks' tails, borax, salt, and musk oil were always sold by his father. While he sat with other men, discussing prices and passing the mouthpiece of a hubble-bubble pipe around and puffing smoke, Shainu's wife and children wandered through the village, feasting their eyes on the wonderful things brought up from the plains of India. Temba had never sat with his father when the selling took place.

Then there was this business of the *memsahib*. Temba had neither seen nor heard of her before. How could he go to such a woman? His heart went cold at the thought. He finally voiced his fears, and Shainu Droma opened his eyes.

"There is nothing to fear, son of mine. I am not going to ask you to buy and sell. You are a strong boy, but you are not wise in the ways of merchants. There are men in Rakfazar Bazaar who would rub their hands and pull hairs from their beards in glee if you went to them to sell our *lac* and musk oil. They would ask you to sit and drink tea, and when you came away they would have robbed you of everything. In the hands of such men you would be like a newborn lamb in the talons of an eagle."

Temba relaxed. When his father talked like that it meant he had already thought of a way out of the difficulties. After a moment or so Shainu spoke again.

"When you reach Rakfazar Bazaar you will seek out a man named Ghulam Ali. He is an old man, an old man with a white beard and moustache; but many years ago I helped him, and he has not forgotten it. He and I are like brothers. Tell him who you are. Tell him what has happened to me. Say that I ask him to sell our goods and buy the things we need, especially a pony. And not least of all, ask him to get a gunsmith to mend the rifle. Then ask him to take you to the *memsahib*. He will do all these things, and gladly. He will get the right price for the *lac* and the yaks' tails, and he will not pay too much for the repair of the rifle or for the pony. He will be like a father to you."

Temba sat for a minute or so letting these things sink deep into his mind. Then he asked, "What do I say to this *memsahib*? This I must be sure of, lest a mistake be made."

"You will grow up to be a wise hillman," said his father approvingly. "Before you leave here you will look again at my injured leg. You will look at it until you can close your eyes and tell her just how it appears. When you meet this *memsahib* you will tell her exactly how these claw wounds look. Tell her it was a snow leopard that did the damage. Tell her that we washed the wounds with hot water. She will then tell you what to do. When she has given her words of wisdom, you will make a present of a sheep to her."

"A whole sheep?" The idea of giving such a valuable present startled Temba.

"A whole sheep," his father said soberly. "If I am made well, then a whole sheep will not have been too big a price to pay."

Temba rose. "I will collect the firewood now. Then you can tell me how many sheep and goats to take, and what——"

"You will not go now," his father said. "The day is part gone, and it is a long march to Rakfazar Bazaar. You could not get there before sunset, and on the lower slopes there are those who would take everything from you, even your life, if they saw you as the day ended."

"I could hurry." For once Temba's anxiety made him

try to overrule his father. "The earlier I get to this *memsahib*, the earlier I can get back to heal your wounds."

"A *man* could hurry," his father agreed. "Alas, you are still only a boy. And can you hurry sheep and goats? Farther down the mountain there will be meadows with rich new grass, and you would need a dozen dogs to keep the flock from scattering. You will have to let them graze. You may not have even one dog, for this one still lies as if he will never run again."

There was no arguing with such wisdom. Temba spent a few minutes with the dog. He rubbed Shar from head to foot, and the big mastiff whined softly yet did not once snap at him. Then he forced the dog to his feet. When he hobbled stiffly a yard or so before lying down again, Temba felt hopeful. Shar was bruised and still very stiff, but he would get well.

Temba spent the rest of the day cutting firewood. He had to make three trips into the valley, for the few trees near the compound had been reduced to little more than skeletons by successive travelers who had arrived toward sunset and without firewood in their packs.

He also brought in blocks of snow to add to the supply already in the compound. There were banks of it here and there, and though the sun was warm enough during the daytime, the temperature dropped to freezing at night, and he was able to cut solid blocks of snow.

At sunset Temba prepared the evening meal. Tough youngster though he was, he was feeling very tired— tired and worried, for his father had lain without speaking most of the day.

With the mutton bubbling in the fire-blackened pot Temba asked his father how he felt.

"Are you feeling better, Father?" he said. "I have put in extra barley with the mutton. Do you smell it?"

"I smell it," his father agreed. "But it is tea I need. There is a fire in my blood, and I need only drink. I shall feel better when the heat of the day has gone."

Temba frowned. The heat of the day had already gone, and the chill of the coming night could already be felt. How strange that his father had not noticed this! He made a full kettle of tea, adding an extra half brick of tea to make the brew stronger. It was very black when Temba dropped in the nub of sour-smelling butter that they preferred to milk and sugar.

Shainu drank several mugs of tea, but made only a pretense of eating. Fever from the poisoned claw slashes had raised his temperature; it would go higher as the poison spread. The one bright spot during that evening meal was the sudden interest Shar took in life when Shainu gave up trying to eat his piece of mutton and threw it toward the dog.

All day the mastiff had lain motionless, but now he came to his feet, and there was some of the old eagerness in the way he gulped down the meat.

Temba was trying to persuade his father that if he smoked a pipe of tobacco he might feel better when the snow leopard reappeared. The piece of mutton she had limped away with that morning was not enough. She had three kittens to feed, and she seemed to have gone for days without a real meal. Quietly she had climbed onto the compound wall.

Shar saw her first, and though he was still stiff-muscled, he did not hesitate. With a fearsome snarl he hurled himself at the wall. Had he not been so stiff and muscle-sore, he might have managed to scale the wall and chase the intruder. But his charge did frighten the snow leopard, for as Temba called him back, she fell, rather than leaped, off the far side of the wall.

It was a bad night for everyone. Temba was afraid to drop off into a deep sleep for fear the fire would die down and allow the snow leopard to return. He could hear the starving animal limping about outside the compound. She was sniffing hungrily, yet afraid to scale the wall again.

The sheep and goats, too, kept waking as the snow leopard's scent reached them, and Shar lay with eyes that kept closing, then opening. He knew the snow leopard was near and, like a good sentry, would be ready for her should she try to attack the flock.

When the first gray began to show behind the Himalayan peaks, Temba stirred the fire to a brighter blaze. He filled the kettle and half-filled the mutton pot with hard-packed snow before adding more mutton. He stirred two handfuls of barley meal into the mutton and one handful into the teakettle. While waiting for the water to heat, he fed the sheep and goats, then chose the ones he would take with him. These he loaded with pannier packs of *lac*, musk oil, and salt. His father had decided not to send either yaks' tails or borax as he had a special customer for those things, from whom he got a very good price.

Instead of the usual breakfast of a mug of tea, Temba had mutton, but his father would only drink tea. After replenishing the mutton pot and making sure that his father had everything close at hand, Temba checked his new weapon. It was a branch he had found the day before—a branch so straight that it had immediately suggested itself as a weapon. By tying his knife onto the end, he made a splendid spear. With this, Temba was sure he could be more than a match for any snow leopard even though his father thought a spear would be of no use.

When he was ready he shook his father gently and told him he was leaving. Shainu lay for half a minute, gathering strength before attempting to turn over so that he could look up at his son. The slightest movement sent crippling shafts of pain through his leg. Noting the anxiety on Temba's face, he made a great effort and found the strength to speak almost gaily. "Wash the fear from your heart, my son. This day you leave your childhood behind. When this journey ends, you will be in Rakfazar Bazaar, and no longer a boy, but a *man*! Remember that, Temba Droma, by sunset you will be a man. Let them all know you are the son of Shainu Droma. When you have sold our goods, visit the *mem-sahib*, then come back to me swiftly. When I hear your voice again I know it will be the voice of a man."

Raising a hand, he laid it for a moment on Temba's arm, then he closed his eyes and sank back. Temba had never heard his father talk like this. There was a wonderful message in his words. He had said that this was to be the last day of Temba's boyhood. By sunset Temba

Droma would be a man. The idea of leaving his childhood behind made the hill boy unconsciously square his
shoulders and stand more upright.

There was no shaking of hands, no words of goodby.
Temba took a final look at his father's wounds so he
would be able to describe them to the *memsahib,* and
then called the dog and heaved aside the brushwood gate.
The old billy goat, the lead animal of the small caravan,
bleated excitedly and trotted out.

Shainu Droma heard the bleating but did not open
his eyes. His whole body seemed to be on fire. His skin
was dry and he felt as if he were floating on air, like
a king vulture. He was at the beginning of a high fever,
though he did not know this, nor did Temba.

Temba was excited and proud as he stepped out of
the compound. His head was filled with the words: "By
sunset you will be a man." Then some of his elation
vanished. Staring at him from a distance of about sixty
yards was the dreaded snow leopard. She had waited all
night for a chance to make a kill.

5
Face
to Face

THE EXCITED BAAING AND BLEATING DIED QUICKLY AS the foremost sheep and goats saw the snow leopard. Their fear was passed on to the flock behind, and for a few seconds there was silence. Had Temba carried a rifle, the end would have been quick and sure, for the snow leopard was coming toward him at a limping trot.

It was the moment for a quick decision. At about ten yards distance the snow leopard hugged the earth and gathered her muscles for a spring. Her eyes were like fire-lit emeralds, and a hard purring came from deep down in her throat.

It was Shar that made her hesitate. Though still bruised and sore he stalked forward, stiff-legged, his hackles up and his lips drawn back in a frightening snarl, to meet the attacker.

For a moment it seemed as if dog and snow leopard would settle the issue at once in single combat. Then Temba raised his homemade spear and threw it. At the same moment he gave a piercing shriek, and the dog bounded forward. The snow leopard turned, snarled, and then scurried away at a limping gallop.

Temba called his dog back, retrieved his spear, and stood for a moment hurling threats at the snow leopard. At a distance she turned and faced him, snarling and holding her injured paw off the ground.

Now free to proceed, the lead billy goat, remembering the rich grass and babbling streams down the valley, rushed for the narrow path that led in the direction of Rakfazar Bazaar. At once the rest of the pannier-laden flock followed him.

Temba dragged the mass of prickly thornbushes back into the compound gateway before following his flock. Once on the narrow path they could not be attacked, for it wound across the side of a steep and stony hill where sheep and goats must walk in single file. No animal could attack them from the side. They—and he—were safe!

In his delight Temba cuffed the dog playfully across the head. "My father spoke the truth when he said that this day I would leave my childhood behind," he told Shar. "I am a man! Only a man could drive off a snow leopard—and do it without a rifle. But you helped, Shar. This night you shall eat mutton until you can eat no more."

Temba was so happy that for the moment even his father's condition did not worry him. For several hours he drove his flock hard, but the sheep and goats did not object for they, too, were eager to get to the valley. Several thousand feet down the hill track Temba let them rest. Here the grass grew bright green with the freshness of spring, and a stream babbled among the stones.

The last lap of the journey was the worst. Temba and his animals were all very tired. Only when they saw thin wisps of smoke rising in the red light of the dying day did they begin to move a little quicker. The smoke was rising from the village called Rakfazar Bazaar.

It hardly deserved the name of village. There were forty houses, and for fifty weeks of the year few visitors ever came that way. But for the other two weeks merchants came up from the plains of India to meet hillmen and their families who had crossed the high passes. The men bought and sold while the women and children wandered about, goggle-eyed in wonder at the things they saw.

There were traders from Chittagong, Madras, Calcutta, and even some from as far away as Bombay. There were hook-nosed Pathans from the Khyber Pass, and an occasional wandering Arab. It was a mixture of honest men and thieves.

For these two exciting weeks the villagers rented their houses to the visiting merchants and went to live in makeshift homes. It was a happy time of buying and selling, eating and drinking. News of the past year was exchanged, for here in the foothills there were no radios or newspapers. The world could be at war, but the hillmen would not know it until they came to the market at Rakfazar Bazaar.

Temba halted his weary flock when they were about a hundred yards from the village street. In the noise and bustle, lights and movement, he was suddenly afraid.

When his father had been explaining what he had to do in Rakfazar Bazaar it had seemed simple. Find the old man, tell him, and all would be well.

If the old man had been waiting to greet Temba all would have been well. But how could he find Ghulam Ali? This his father had not told him. Visitors to Rakfazar Bazaar outnumbered villagers by ten to one. Lost in a great crowd, with no one to tell him what to do or where to go, Temba felt like a small boy. Fear made his stomach feel cold and empty. He was tempted to turn back and sleep that night away from the village. In daylight it would be easier to find Ghulam Ali.

Then Temba remembered his father's leg. Anxiety for Shainu outweighed his fear of entering Rakfazar Bazaar. Frightened though he was, Temba knew he must go on and find the old man.

Slowly and carefully he tied his flock in line, nose to tail. It was a precaution he had seen his father take, for Shainu Droma did not trust the crowds in the village street. He had often warned his son to keep a keen eye open for *loosewallahs* (thieves). In such a crowd there were long-fingered men who could steal a sheep or a goat in the twinkling of an eye.

Nor were there any policemen to keep order. At sunset the women went to their tents, and as night fell, even the hillmen kept a hand on their clumsy purses. When the stall keepers lighted their little lamps the place became a mixture of tiny pools of yellow light and large areas of deep shadow. It was not unknown for a caravan to start at one end of the street with twenty sheep and goats and march out at the other end with only eighteen. An animal could be hustled out of line, dragged around behind the nearest house and there killed and skinned in a matter of minutes. By the time the indignant hillman began a search, his missing goat or sheep might be simmering gently over a stall keeper's charcoal brazier—and who could identify a lump of mutton in a steaming pan?

Even with his flock linked together, Temba was uneasy. He led them into the thronged street and pushed a way through to the *maidan*—a small piece of grazing land—at its end. It was there that the hillmen pitched their tents. Once on the *maidan* Temba knew his animals would be reasonably safe, for the hill people were honest, and few visitors wandered into the camp after nightfall.

Had he not been so worried about his flock and about his father, Temba would have found the scene fascinating. Each of the temporary stalls had its own candle or oil lamp, which lighted up the colorful clothing and cast shadows all about. Nailed on top of many of the stalls were crude pictures of the all-seeing Eye of Buddha. One stall keeper, whose home was in faraway Bombay, had a model of the elephant god Ganash hanging over his wares. Stray dogs slunk about, looking for a chance to snatch a mouthful of food, and were kicked out of the way by anyone near enough to get a foot to them.

Men sat about in little groups, some passing around the mouthpiece of a hubble-bubble pipe, taking a few puffs before handing the "smoke" over to his neighbor. Others squatted before food stalls where men cooked rice and mutton, or made tea, or flattened the dough from which the leathery *chappatis* (flat bread cakes) were made before dropping them onto a fire-heated plate to cook.

The air was thick with a variety of appetizing smells that made Temba's nostrils twitch and reminded him that he had walked all day and eaten nothing since early morning. Yet he never allowed his attention to wander from his string of goats and sheep. His dog brought up the rear, snarling a warning to any who came too near, and snapping at stray dogs that came to sniff.

Finally they were through the village street, and looking ahead to the *maidan* with its tents of the hillmen. There were also a few tents belonging to merchants who had been unable to rent a house. Here the darkness was less intense, for at least a score of cooking fires were burning. Pots were bubbling and shadowy figures bent over them, testing the dish or adding a handful of barley meal to thicken the soup. The air was alive with the noise of children, playing and waiting for the evening meal.

Temba found a spot that suited him, and while the sheep and goats sank gratefully down to rest their thin legs, he went over to the stream with his cooking pan. Because of the stream that ran through the *maidan* the grass was always thick and green. Temba's flock would have liked to graze here, but the young hill boy was afraid to free them. Opening a bale of mountain hay he spread it around, then prepared his own meal. He built a fire and put the cooking pot with water from the stream in the fire. Then he added mutton and barley meal to the water.

Temba was unaware that his movements were being watched by a Hindu squatting on the edge of the patch of grass. This man was different from the men in Rakfazar Bazaar. Most hillmen and villagers were powerfully built, with clear eyes and faces burned brick red by the winds that blew off the Himalayan snows. The Hindu was short and fat, with a dark chocolate complexion. He looked as if he ate too much and worked too little. He had a black moustache, which he was forever stroking, but his chin and cheeks were shaved as smooth as polished ivory. His dress, too, was different from the hillmen's whose garments were of handwoven wool, dyed brilliant colors. The Hindu wore white cotton, and it was so clean that it stood out like new snow.

The Hindu's white cap marked him as a man of importance. So did his slippers, which were of beautifully soft leather, dyed red and decorated with ornamental brass wire. On his left wrist he wore a gold watch, with an expanding metal bracelet also of gold and so highly polished that in the daytime it gleamed in the sun. Among the rough, brawny hillmen and the poor villagers —even among the merchants—the Hindu stood out, giving the impression of being a man of wealth.

To look like a rich man was part of the Hindu's stock-in-trade. He was not a rich man at all. He was a crook, a confidence trickster who made his money at these annual bazaars where victims were not difficult to find. He had a smooth tongue, and many times in the past had been able to persuade men to part with their hard-earned rupees with a story of a wonderful rifle he had for sale or some other thing that would make life easier for them.

He was very clever and had never been caught in his trickery.

He had been looking for a likely victim when he saw Temba leading his flock through the crowded Rakfazar Bazaar street. The Hindu had noted their weariness and his eyes had narrowed when he saw that the boy seemed to be alone. He followed, not getting too close and keeping a careful eye open for the boy's relatives. Surely no hill boy ever came alone to Rakfazar Bazaar with a caravan of sheep and goats!

His interest increased as he watched Temba make a small cooking fire, fill his pan from the stream, and then spread hay for his flock. He watched the boy put mutton into the pan. There was not enough mutton for a family —the boy was cooking only for himself!

The Hindu made no move until he saw Temba squat by the fire, dig his knife into the pot, spear a piece of mutton, and begin to eat. Then the Hindu decided that Fortune was smiling on him. This hill boy *was* alone! The Hindu's eyes glistened as he counted the sheep and goats, *and* the panniers of trade goods they had carried.

He took a last cautious look around the *maidan*, for he did not want to be caught by an angry father or uncle. Then he got up, smoothed his white clothes, and decided to try his luck. The other hill people were busy and no one was looking.

Striding briskly across to Temba's fire he stood looking down for a moment at the youngster, then asked, "Boy, is your father looking for me?"

His mouth half filled with hot mutton, Temba looked

up. He chewed for a few moments, studying his visitor. For one wild moment he wondered if the stranger could be the Ghulam Ali who was a friend of his father's—the man who, his father had said, would be glad to help him sell the merchandise, buy a pony, and even take him to the *memsahib*. This first hope died quickly. Shainu Droma had said that Ghulam Ali was an old man, with a white beard and moustache. This sleek man, on whose well-shaved cheeks the firelight glimmered, must be a stranger.

"My father is not here," Temba said, chewing stolidly and hoping the intruder would go away.

"You mean he is not coming here?" the Hindu asked, struggling to keep the excitement from his voice. "Then you must be here with an uncle or an older brother." He must be absolutely certain the boy was alone before he tried any of his confidence tricks. Hillmen were quick to draw a knife, or even lift a rifle, if they discovered they were being cheated.

"I wait for no one," Temba said, and when the Hindu asked the reason, he gave a quick, short answer: "I look after my own business. Don't you have any business to look after?" Temba intended this as a strong hint that the man should go away; instead, it gave the Hindu just the opening he was looking for.

Quietly, even politely, he said: "Boy, I *am* here on business. I am the Government officer who collects the taxes. Everyone who comes here must pay twenty rupees. It is the usual tax to be paid by all who come to Rakfazar Bazaar."

In the act of chewing off another piece of mutton from the piece skewered on his knife blade, Temba paused. Twenty rupees! He knew little of money, for his father handled all the money. Nor did Temba know anything about Government officers and taxes. Whatever business had to be done, Shainu Droma had always done it. He sold their yaks' tails, *lac*, salt, borax, and anything else they brought. He also held the money in a heavy leather purse. Even Temba's mother seldom touched money. When she went shopping, Shainu Droma was by her side to see that no man cheated her, and to pay over, after careful counting, every single rupee she spent.

Never doubting for a moment that the fat man was a Government officer whose duty it was to collect taxes, Temba said more respectfully, "I am sorry, sir, but there can be no payment until tomorrow. I came here only after sunset. I have had no time to sell anything. Tomorrow I seek out my father's friend Ghulam Ali who will sell for me. Then there will be twenty rupees for you."

The Hindu hesitated for a moment. One had to be careful in a small place like Rakfazar Bazaar. On the other hand, if he hesitated, he might lose what could be a splendid prize.

"How long have you known this Ghulam Ali?" he asked. It was important to discover if this boy had many friends among the villagers. To have friends here was unusual, but not impossible.

A moment later the Hindu knew that this *was* his great opportunity, for Temba shook his head and admitted, "I do not know him. He is my father's friend, and I am to seek him out. Perhaps you can tell me where I can find him."

The Hindu shook his head. He must stop this boy from finding anyone who would befriend him. Sadly he said, "You may seek him, boy, but you will never find him. This Ghulam Ali is dead. It was cholera, the quick death; and of course he had no family."

When he saw the dismay in Temba's eyes, he was certain that the boy had no one else to turn to for help. But to make sure he asked, "Have you no other friends? Surely there is someone who could help you."

"No one." The idea that this stranger might be lying to him never crossed Temba's mind. He was suddenly filled with anxiety. With Ghulam Ali dead, what could he do about selling their goods? And who would take him to the *memsahib*?

6
A Trap Set
for Temba

"HM!" THE HINDU RUBBED HIS CHIN GENTLY AND PRE-tended to think. In the red glow of the small cooking fire his eyes were gleaming. If he could get his hands on this boy's possessions there would be no need to stay here longer than the time it took to sell them.

After a pause, during which Temba waited anxiously, the Hindu said, "It is not part of my work to befriend every boy who comes here, but I like your looks. Tell me how it is you are alone."

Temba hesitated. His father had told him that there were always some men at Rakfazar Bazaar who were thieves; yet this man neither looked nor sounded the way Temba thought a thief should look or sound. The thieves they had encountered in the hill passes had been wild-looking men, men who would murder for a sheep.

"My father was hurt by a snow leopard," Temba be-gan and, once started, told the whole story of their en-counter with the snow leopard who had kittens and was limping because of a foot injury. When he told of the damaged Lee-Enfield rifle he had brought in to be repaired, the Hindu could scarcely believe his luck. Not only would he get sheep and goats and panniers of produce but, if he was clever enough, he might even get a Lee-Enfield rifle. It seemed too good to be true!

When Temba finished his story, the Hindu nodded to show his sympathy. Laying a hand lightly on the hill boy's shoulder he said, "A good boy should be given all possible help, Temba Droma, and I am going to do what I can for you. Tomorrow I will help you sell your merchandise. Being a tax officer I know everyone. I might even be able to get a gunsmith to repair the rifle. Is it badly damaged? Let me see it."

Temba unwrapped the rifle and stirred the fire so that it gave a little more light. Rifles were not new to the Hindu, and it needed no more than a glance to tell him that a good gunsmith would be able to repair this rifle in an hour or so. Its value was obvious to him. British army rifles had always been precious, for the Lee-Enfield shot true. Since the British departure from India such magnificent weapons grew scarcer every year. This was indeed his lucky day!

Rising with the Lee-Enfield still in his right hand, the Hindu said, "I will take this to a friend who is a gunsmith. Once he has examined it he will . . ." and there he stopped, his mouth gaping in shocked surprise. Temba had moved like lightning. He grabbed the rifle and with a savage jerk snatched it from the Hindu's grasp.

"This is Shainu Droma's rifle," he said sternly. "*I must*

take it to the gunsmith. When Shainu Droma dies this rifle will become mine. So it is not given to any man, except by me."

For a moment the Hindu was tempted to bluster and threaten. But realizing that this hill boy would not be easily frightened, he held his tongue. The boy had the hill people's directness of thought and words; he would have to be handled with cunning.

"I only thought to save time," he explained smoothly, an apologetic smile on his fat face. "But it is right that a son should look after his father's rifle. You are a son any father would be proud of." Patting Temba on the shoulder again, he pretended he did not see the suspicious scowl on the hill boy's face. "Now I must go, for I have many duties to perform; I will return at sunrise and take you to a gunsmith. With your father badly hurt you will not wish to stay in Rakfazar Bazaar a minute longer than is necessary, eh? Oh . . . one other thing. Tell no one that I have not collected the tax from you, or every other hillman will think I should do the same for him." Then, smiling in as fatherly a way as he knew how, the Hindu left.

Temba watched until darkness had swallowed the man. Then he slowly rewrapped the damaged rifle in the oily rags. He was worried. He did not like accepting help from a stranger, but the news that Ghulam Ali was dead had been an unexpected blow. He had to have someone to help him sell their goods, advise about the repair of the rifle, and take him to the *memsahib*. As he sat down to eat more mutton, he reluctantly decided he would have to accept the tax collector's offer.

Meanwhile, the Hindu was hurrying off on his "important business." Already he was thinking up a plan to get his hands on everything Temba Droma possessed. At a street stall he purchased a plate of rice and mutton and a cup of tea to wash it down. As he ate, he worked out the details of his scheme. By the time he left the stall every smallest detail was arranged in his mind. The only thing to do now was to find the right partner to help him.

He wandered through the crowded street, peering at small groups of men squatting before teamakers' stalls, past places where the smell of mutton and goat meat told of a food stall. But he knew that the man he wanted would not be eating, for he must be almost penniless.

The Hindu found Nasir Ali, the gunsmith he was looking for, squatting in a tattered tent outside the village. Here men gathered to drink *rakshi*, a fiery liquor made from fermented rice. Nasir Ali's face was drawn into a deep scowl, and the mug in his hand contained only a few drops of *rakshi*. Other men kept drinking, but Nasir Ali only pretended to drink. Trade had never been so bad for him. Most of the caravans had arrived, and no one seemed to need a new rifle or to have old rifles to be repaired.

The Hindu knew the gun trade was poor, and that Nasir Ali would snatch at any chance to earn a few rupees. After recognizing the gunsmith the Hindu crept around, and kneeling behind him whispered, "I know where a man who is skilled in rifles could earn two hundred rupees. If you are interested, join me outside." Then the Hindu rose and strolled out.

Nasir Ali turned his head for a moment, so that he

would recognize the speaker. He shrugged and pretended to listen to what a rug man from Bukara was saying. Nasir Ali *was* interested in earning rupees, but he knew is was bad business to be too eager. The fat Hindu would wait. After several minutes had passed, Nasir Ali drained the few drops of *rakshi* in his mug and wandered out into the village street. He did not stand and stare, but walked off, pausing to look first at one stall and then another. Eventually the Hindu sidled up, as Nasir Ali had known he would, and plucked gently at the gunsmith's sleeve. "I will see you in your shop," he whispered.

Even then Nasir Ali did not hurry, although the very thought of picking up such a sum as the Hindu had mentioned—two hundred rupees—made the gunsmith's eyes glitter. Yet one had to be careful. He had seen the Hindu before at various bazaars in the foothills of the Himalayas, and he knew that behind that fat, often smiling face was a cunning brain.

"He does not offer two hundred rupees unless the work is too dangerous for him," Nasir Ali decided. "He is as slippery as a water snake and as dangerous as a king cobra. I will have to watch him. Yet I would be a fool not to take a chance. With two hundred rupees in my pouch I could fill my belly for weeks. I must have money, or I will starve."

Having thus decided, Nasir Ali stalked through the crowd to the tumbledown house he had rented for the period of the Bazaar. It held his portable forge, the big box containing his tools, and a few rifles he hoped to sell. Lighting his lamp he sat down and waited. Within a minute the Hindu arrived.

Nasir Ali picked up a pair of tongs and a rifle as if he were about to begin a repair job. With hardly more than a sidelong glance at the Hindu he asked curtly, "What is this business you mentioned? You talked of a fee of two hundred rupees. Out with it, for as you know I am a busy man with little time to spare."

He was answered with a contemptuous: "Tell that to the hillmen if you like, but not to me. I have seen you wandering around like a homeless dog, glad to turn and snap if someone offered to buy you a dish of mutton and rice. You are not a busy man."

"If you have a job for me, let me know it," Nasir Ali snarled. "It is true that for the moment business is not good. Tomorrow I am expecting——" and there the Hindu stopped him.

"I know where there is a beautiful English rifle—a Lee-Enfield."

"I have a Lee-Enfield rifle," Nasir Ali snapped. "You spoke of two hundred rupees. If you are joking with me, fat one, I——"

Interrupting Nasir Ali the Hindu said, "If you are interested, I can promise you maybe more than two hundred rupees."

Nasir Ali's reply was brief. "I have always been interested in rupees," he said. "Now, cunning jackal, tell me the whole story. If you are offering me two hundred rupees or more it is to do something you are afraid to do."

The Hindu told Nasir Ali the story he had heard from Temba. When Nasir Ali merely stared, the Hindu went on persuasively, "The boy is innocent as a newborn babe. If we work together we could take everything. And remember, there are other sheep and goats left with the boy's father. It will not be difficult. I have everything planned."

Nasir Ali pondered, plucking idly at the long hairs of his straggly moustache. When he still made no comment, the Hindu threw in the last rich bait: "There is something else. The boy told me the snow leopard that injured his father was nursing young."

"*Humph*!"

"There are at least two kittens," the Hindu pointed out, "and the boy knows where they are hidden. What price will snow leopard kittens bring from the man who buys wild animals?"

Nasir Ali had already decided to work with the Hindu, but this latest piece of information made his eyes gleam.

Snow leopards, especially young ones that could be tamed, would indeed bring a good price. There were always men looking for animals for the zoos of Western Europe or the United States of America.

"I shall listen to your plan," he said, "but it must be foolproof. You know what manner of men these hill folk are. If you cheat, and are caught, you are likely to die quickly."

"I, too, know the hillmen," the Hindu agreed. "Nor do I wish to die. My plan is good and cannot fail. Listen."

Nasir Ali listened, and slowly the skeptical frown changed to a grin of appreciation. He tried to see a weak place in the scheme, but could not. It seemed completely foolproof. Eventually he agreed to help, and on the strength of their partnership borrowed five rupees, which the Hindu handed over reluctantly. Then the gunsmith was told to put out his light and stay in his workshop for a few minutes.

"I will go out first. It is better that we are not seen together," the Hindu explained. "I shall bring the hill boy here with the rifle soon after sunrise. You will pretend not to want to do the work, then will agree for my sake. That will help the boy believe I am his friend."

"How can a man be born with such cunning?" Nasir Ali asked, grinning. "One day you will have rupees by the *lakh* (100,000)—if someone has not slit your fat throat before then."

"Until tomorrow," the Hindu said, hurriedly leaving.

In his camp on the *maidan* Temba catnapped throughout the night. He was worried about his father and uneasy about their little flock and the panniers of goods stacked by the fire. The village was quiet now and the lights had disappeared. On the grass a score of red spots showed where fires, covered with turf, smoldered. Temba had not damped down his fire. He wanted to be able to see that all was well, and each time the embers began to fall in on themselves he opened his eyes, got up, and added a few more sticks.

With the first gray of dawn the camp came to life. The

women appeared from their black tents and kneeling before their slumbering fires they blew them to sparkling life. When the flames were leaping they took their fire-blackened kettles to the stream. Temba followed their example. At the stream he stood for a minute or so listening to their gossip. There was much laughter and chatter, for this yearly visit to Rakfazar Bazaar was the only real occasion most of them had to meet other women. Temba wished he had someone to talk to, but the children had not come from the tents, and a hill boy does not speak to strange women.

He filled his cooking pot, then knelt by the stream and splashed a handful of water onto his face. With his face still dripping, he returned to his cooking fire. When the water began to boil, Temba broke half a tea brick into the pan, then added some barley meal and a piece of butter.

Before Temba had finished his second mugful, the Hindu arrived, looking even more resplendent in the morning sun. His newly laundered clothes were white as snow, and his smooth-shaved chin gleamed as if it had been oiled. He believed that a well-shaved, well-dressed man inspired confidence among ill-dressed, unwashed hill people.

Marching straight over to Temba's little camp, he gave the boy a quick salutation, then suggested they should move off at once. "Stack your goods by the fire. They will be safe enough. We all know that hill people are honest."

"Even so, I shall tether the sheep and goats," Temba insisted. "It is better that they do not mix with the flocks of other people. Could I argue with a grown man, if one of my sheep or goats began to graze with his? I shall water them and give them hay; then they will be content."

"But you must hurry," the Hindu insisted. "I have sought out a gunsmith; he is a very busy man, but he has agreed to look at your rifle. If we do not go immediately he may begin work on something else and your chance will be lost."

"A man cannot leave his flock thirsty and hungry," Temba explained. "If they die, he becomes no more than a beggar. I shall hurry; fear not."

The Hindu was fuming as he waited for Temba to take the sheep and goats to the stream. In an effort to save time he cut open a bale of the mountain hay and helped Temba spread it when the flock had had its fill of water.

Temba tried the Hindu's patience once more with the suggestion that they should first go to see the *memsahib*. "Once I know what to do to help my father I shall be happier," he explained.

If the prize he was working for had not been so great, the Hindu would have cursed the hill boy and gone away. But with a great effort he controlled his temper.

"There are many things a hill boy cannot possibly understand," he told Temba. "One of them is that this *memsahib* will not have eaten yet. White people do not begin the day as we do when the sun rises. By the time we have been to see the gunsmith she may have gone to her tent, but she will certainly not be giving medicine or advice yet."

"But if we are there when she begins work," Temba

insisted, "we shall not have to wait. There may be many wishing to see her."

Once again curbing his temper with difficulty, the Hindu said, "All right, we shall do that, but now we must hurry. There is much to do. Besides seeing the *memsahib*, there is the rifle to be mended and a pony to be bought. Come on."

"There is also the matter of payment for the *memsahib*," Temba said, remembering what his father had told him. "What shall I take—a sheep or a goat?"

"Take nothing." By this time the Hindu's temper was almost in shreds. "In some ways these white people are mad. This woman will take payment if you offer it, but if you have nothing she will still give you advice and medicine. Perhaps you could offer payment later. She will not be angry."

Temba could not understand anyone doing work for nothing, but he picked up the damaged rifle, still wrapped in oily rags, and followed the Hindu off the *maidan* and across to the village street. The single street of Rakfazar Bazaar was already beginning to buzz with life. Stall keepers had uncovered their wares. The village men who sold tea, *chapattis*, mutton, goat meat, and the piled heaps of boiled snowy rice were blowing their charcoal braziers from a glow to white heat as the first customers of the day began to arrive. During the two weeks of the Rakfazar Bazaar the hill people had to do a year's selling and buying, so for them every minute of each day was precious.

At any other time Temba would have dallied to feast

his eyes on the wonderful things to be seen—piles of trinkets to delight the heart of any hill woman, gleaming wire bangles, heaps of glittering blue, yellow, and red glass beads. Copper-coated kettles gleamed richly in the sun. A stall laden with many rolls of dazzling silks had already attracted a score of round-eyed women and girls, who stood about admiring the material, fingering it, and whispering to one another. At another stall there was a display of wonderful knives, large and small, which would make any hill boy's eyes shine with envy.

The sharp smell of curried rice made Temba sniff appreciatively, but he did not hesitate. Once, when the Hindu slowed his pace to call a greeting to someone, Temba plucked at his sleeve. The Hindu had told him that the *memsahib*'s tent was on the far side of the village, and Temba wanted to get there before anyone else.

7
"We Must Not Let Him Die"

SOME DISTANCE BEYOND THE VILLAGE, AWAY FROM ITS hubbub and smell, several khaki-colored tents were pitched by the side of a mountain rill. Waiting for the *memsahib* were more than forty women; many had been there throughout the night. Most of them carried babies on their hips, and some also had older children with them.

The Hindu did not lead Temba to the end of the line, but marched boldly to the head. There were angry murmurs from those who had been waiting for hours, but the Hindu looked like such an important man that the murmurs died away. Half an hour later the tent flaps were opened and the day's work began.

It was nine o'clock when Temba rather fearfully obeyed the beckoning finger of a bearded Sikh orderly and went into the tent. The Hindu followed at Temba's heels. He showed no sign of uneasiness, but it was a never-to-be-forgotten moment for the hill boy. For the first time in his life Temba was close enough to touch a *memsahib*, and he gazed at her with awe-filled eyes.

Sitting at a small table she looked so clean as to appear unnatural. She was dressed in plain khaki overalls, and her forearms were covered to the wrists with dazzling white cuffs. Her head, too, was covered with a queer white cap. If she had suddenly pointed a finger at Temba he would have fled, but she smiled at him. That was something Temba had not expected, and he would have remained in awe-struck silence if the Hindu had not nudged him sharply in the back.

"Tell her what is wrong, boy," the Hindu whispered. "Don't waste her time."

Temba was flustered, but to his amazement the white woman spoke to him in his own language. Smiling, she asked him to tell her everything. Temba was suddenly calm again. Quickly he told the *memsahib* of the snow leopard and of his father's wounds. She asked him what the claw injuries looked like, and the smile faded when he described them.

"And is your father in great pain when he puts his foot on the ground? Does he feel hot? And does he want much to drink and nothing to eat?"

That frightened Temba. How could she know these things, for they were just how his father was. Seeing the fear in his eyes, the white woman smiled and said quietly, "Boy, there is nothing to fear. I understand how these things look because I have seen other men who have been hurt by leopards. Such wounds are always the same."

She then asked him the exact location of the little

camp where Shainu Droma lay. Temba could answer
that easily, but when he said it had taken him all the
previous day to come down the pass to Rakfazar Bazaar
the *memsahib*'s lips pressed to a thin line. Turning to her
Sikh orderly, and speaking in English, she said, "It
sounds to me as if this camp could be five or six thousand
feet up from here. Could we get men from the village to
bring the injured man down?"

The orderly's reply was a slow but decisive shake of
the head. "The people are too busy, *memsahib*. An injured man means nothing to them."

Then the white woman asked Temba, "Have you any
relatives or friends who could bring your father from
his camp to me?"

The Hindu at Temba's side did not give the hill boy
a chance to answer. With a sad shake of his head he
murmured, "I am afraid there is no one, *memsahib*. I am
here with the boy because I talked to him last night,
realized he was alone, and felt sorry for him. Perhaps if
you could give him something with which to dress the
wounds he might take a pony up the pass and try to bring
his father down. That is the only thing I can suggest. I
might go with the boy, if . . ." His voice trailed off as he
noticed Temba eyeing him suspiciously.

The white woman thanked the Hindu, then turned to
her Sikh orderly and gave him instructions regarding
medical supplies he was to pack for Temba to take. To
Temba she said, "Listen carefully, for what I tell you
may save your father's life." She explained how dirt under the claws of any wild animal could start blood poisoning in anyone suffering from claw wounds. But she

said there were ways of killing the poison, and when her orderly laid a small bottle and a box of ointment on the table, she explained to Temba what they were for. The tablets would reduce Shainu Droma's high temperature —take the fire out of his blood. The ointment would kill the poison. She added a roll of thin pink cloth, or lint, a packet of silvery safety pins, and two rolls of three-inch-wide bandages.

The tablets were to be given to Shainu Droma every four hours. Then the orderly demonstrated for Temba how a wound was cleansed and covered with the lint smeared with ointment before being bound in place by a bandage.

As Temba reached out for the tablets the white woman took hold of his hand. It was ingrained with dirt. Without a word she led him into the back part of the tent, poured water into a bowl, and with soap and brush scrubbed his hands and arms up to the elbow. Then she told Temba to repeat the washing. Even when he had finished, his palms still looked dirty, but the white woman smiled.

"Know this, hill boy," she told Temba, "you have scrubbed a thousand devils off your hands! They hide in the dirt, and if they got into your father's injured leg, nothing could save him. Before you touch your father's leg, before you give him one of the white tablets or open the box of magic ointment, your hands must be as clean as they are now. See, I will give you a piece of soap and a towel. Have clean hands when you tend your father's wounds . . . and he may recover. If your hands are dirty, he will surely die. The devils in the dirt can kill him."

Returning to the front part of the tent, she wrapped

the ointment, lint, tablets, bandages and safety pins in with the soap and towel. Handing the supplies to Temba, she said, "You know now what to do for your father, but if it is possible, bring him in so that I can have him in my little hospital. Blood poisoning from wild animal scratches usually needs skilled treatment. But you must get to him quickly and tend his wounds to save his life." Then, with a smile, she nodded to the orderly who ushered the Hindu and the hill boy out into the sunshine.

Temba had the damaged rifle tucked under his right arm. The medical supplies wrapped in the towel were in his left hand. He was trying desperately to remember everything the *memsahib* had said and his head buzzed with all the things they had to do, so that he was glad to let the Hindu take command.

"Now to the gunsmith," the Hindu said pompously. "Without a good rifle no one can face a starving snow leopard. Once——"

"But the money!" Temba interrupted. Young though he was, he knew that no one could do business in Rakfazar Bazaar without money. "Should we not sell some of the pannier packs—the salt and musk oil or some *lac*? And did you not say I must pay twenty rupees tax?"

In his plans the Hindu had forgotten the "government tax" he had talked of the previous evening. But he had always been able to tell a quick lie. Patting Temba gently on the shoulder he said, "Do not worry about the tax. I paid it. When I talked with you last night I knew that you were an honest boy. You can repay me later. However, you are right about needing money, and we will sell some of your merchandise. Then, as soon as the rifle is repaired, you must get to your father quickly. He must be very ill now—very ill." He shot a quick glance at Temba to see how he took that worrying thought.

Temba's mouth drooped. He had felt happier when the *memsahib* was telling him how to doctor Shainu Droma's injured leg. Now the Hindu's words reminded him that a day and a half would soon have passed since he left the compound in the hills. He nodded agreement. "Yes, we must hurry. It will take a day to reach Shainu Droma. We must not let him die."

They pushed their way through the crowded street to the *maidan*, packed the panniers on the sheep and goats, and drove them off to a merchant. The Hindu had no difficulty in selling everything. He did not haggle over the price as Temba's father would have done. If Temba had not protested, the Hindu would have sold the sheep and goats as well.

"Not these. None of them," Temba insisted desperately. "In the hills they are our food and clothing. We get milk from them, wool for clothing, and when other things are scarce we can kill a sheep or a goat for food. My father would never sell them."

So the sheep and goats were herded back to the *maidan* where once again Temba tethered them and left the mastiff to keep guard. Save for the slightest of limps, Shar seemed to have completely recovered from his fall over the cliff. No thief would get away with either a sheep or a goat while he was on guard.

A hundred yards up the hillside a temporary enclosure

had been made for the dozen shaggy mountain ponies that had been brought in for sale. They were sturdy, thickset beasts, not beautiful, not comfortable to ride, but tremendously strong and surefooted. What was more, they were accustomed to the bitter weather and the thin mountain air, and they never shied at the dangerous stony tracks of the passes.

Normally the buying of a pony could take a day. The animal would be put through its paces, its teeth examined, and a score of other tests made before the haggling began. This day made history for the Tibetan dealer. Temba looked at the ponies, decided which one he wanted, and asked the price. When the dealer began by saying that Temba had chosen the best of the lot, the Hindu interrupted with a pompous, "The price, man, the price? You have been asked how many rupees you want for him."

The dealer's eyes goggled. Sure that this well-dressed man would try to beat down the price, he asked far more than he expected to get. To his utter amazement Temba agreed at once. The moment the dealer had bitten each coin and rung it on a stone to make sure it was not a bad one, the deal was complete.

Temba would have trotted with the pony to the gunsmith's if the Hindu had not objected to such undignified speed. They passed around behind the crowded village street, and almost caught Nasir Ali off guard.

The gunsmith was in a bad temper, for he had expected the Hindu to bring the hill boy and the rifle soon after sunrise and it was now three hours after dawn. He was standing in the doorway of his hired workshop, a black scowl on his face, when he saw the Hindu, Temba, and the pony. Hurrying inside, the gunsmith worked his bellows furiously, blowing his fire to a white heat. When his visitors called from the doorway he was just taking a strip of glowing metal from his fire. He did not even look up as they walked in, but began hammering away at the metal until its glowing pink changed to blue. Only then did he look up.

This little piece of play-acting was for Temba's benefit, to convince him that the gunsmith was a very busy man. Nodding to his visitors, Nasir Ali placed the cooling strip of metal back in the fire, wiped his brow, and laid down the hammer and pincers.

"We want you to repair this," the Hindu said, taking the damaged rifle from Temba and handing it to the gunsmith.

Nasir Ali took the two parts, but his eyes were on the breechwork and barrel of the Lee-Enfield. He squinted through the barrel, and his heart leaped with joy. Here was a weapon that had been very well cared for. It was a rifle that would surely fire straight. He tried the bolt, and that gave a very satisfying sound to his experienced ears. To straighten the bent metalwork and refit the butt would take only a few hours.

Giving the anxious Temba a quick glance, he nodded, then laid the rifle on his makeshift workbench. "I can do it. Come back a week today, and it will be like new."

"But I want it today," Temba blurted out. "I must be on my way up the pass this afternoon."

"Oh-oh-oh-oh-oh-ho-ho-ho!" Nasir Ali threw back his head and laughed, and his loud guffaws beat on Temba's ears like thunder.

"You cannot do it today?" Temba interrupted him angrily.

"I could do it this morning," Nasir Ali said, pretending to wipe tears of laughter from his eyes, "but I won't. Who do you think you are, boy, to come here and expect me to put aside all my work just for you? No, come back in a week and . . ." and there he stopped, for Temba had stepped forward and picked up the rifle.

This was a move neither of the men had expected. The Hindu caught Temba by the arm and whispered urgently, "Do not do anything rash; there is no other gunsmith in the village."

"I must start for the pass now," Temba said. "Since he cannot do the work for a week, I must take the damaged rifle with me."

"Wait, I will talk to him," the Hindu said, trying to soothe Temba. "Go outside for a minute or so. I cannot let you go up the pass to face that *shaitan* of a snow leopard without a gun of some kind. Have patience. Maybe I can borrow a rifle for you."

Temba went out. He spent the next few minutes examining the pony he had bought. It was a splendid animal, and the hill boy was sure it would be able to carry his injured father down the mountain without difficulty. Then the Hindu called him in. He was smiling and rubbing his hands as if he had just completed a splendid piece of business.

"I have told the gunsmith everything," he said. "About your father and the snow leopard, and how the *memsahib* says your father must be brought down to Rakfazar Bazaar immediately. He is a kindly man and has agreed to lend you his own rifle——"

"On condition that you go with him," Nasir Ali interrupted. "I would be a fool to take a damaged weapon and let you go off with my own fine rifle . . . !"

"Yes, yes, yes," the Hindu agreed. "I have said that you will pay ten rupees for the loan of the rifle," the Hindu told Temba, "and I have promised to accompany you up the pass." When Temba looked at him suspiciously, he added hastily, "to make sure that the gunsmith's rifle is brought back."

Temba had had no experience with liars, for in the hills men spoke only the truth. Suddenly all his troubles seemed to be melting away like spring snow. From the leather purse he carried under his coat he counted out ten rupees for Nasir Ali.

"Now I must go back to the *maidan* to find some hill woman to look after my flock while I am away," he said.

"Can't the dog do that?" The Hindu did not want a savage hill dog with them when they started up the pass. He hated dogs.

"Can a dog untether sheep and goats so they can go to the stream for water? Can he open a bale of hay? No, I must find a woman to do this, but the dog will stay to watch the flock. No woman would do that; she has other things to do."

Temba hurried off, leaving the Hindu still at Nasir

Ali's. A hill woman camping on the *maidan* was persuaded to feed and water the flock for the two days Temba expected to be away.

At Nasir Ali's the Hindu and the gunsmith were making last-minute arrangements. "This rifle that Temba borrows must be a rifle that will not fire," the Hindu insisted. "You know what these hill people are like. If the boy discovered we were tricking him he would turn around and shoot me without a moment's hesitation. You must see that the weapon is no good."

Nasir Ali frowned thoughtfully. "I have some faulty ammunition," he suggested, "but the danger is that while most cartridges misfire, some of them are good."

"We can't risk a mistake," the Hindu insisted, his worry bringing a thin dappling of sweat to his forehead. "Surely there must be some way of fixing a rifle so that it won't fire. You say you are a good gunsmith, and——"

"I *am* a good gunsmith," Nasir Ali snorted, "but where guns are concerned these hill people aren't fools. But I think I can do it."

"How? There must be no chance of a slip."

"I have a rifle bolt with a broken firing pin," Nasir Ali explained. "I'll put that bolt in the rifle I lend him. With a broken firing pin the rifle will be no better than a walking stick. You will be safe, even if he isn't," he ended, grinning.

They went over the details of the plan, but there was an unexpected snag when Temba returned. After telling them that he had arranged about the flock and the dog and had got feed for the pony, he picked up the rifle

Nasir Ali was lending him and said he would test it. Disaster faced the gunsmith and the Hindu. Nasir Ali snatched the weapon back, pretending to be furious that anyone would doubt one of his rifles.

"But what use is a rifle if the man who fires it does not know its little tricks?" Temba protested. "I have heard my father say that some rifles fire a little high, some to the left, some to the right. How am I to kill this snow leopard if I do not know my rifle?"

By this time Nasir Ali had whipped out the damaged rifle bolt and slipped it into his pocket. It was an old custom never to leave a rifle bolt in, for there were still gun thieves about, but a rifle without a bolt was hardly worth stealing.

Winking meaningly at Nasir Ali, the Hindu pleaded that Temba was right and that he should be allowed to try the rifle. The talk gave Nasir Ali an opportunity to substitute a good bolt for the damaged one. Still grumbling and pretending that his honor had been smeared by the suggestion that he might lend a rifle that did not fire straight, the gunsmith handed Temba the weapon.

A stone was set up behind the house at a range of fifty yards. Temba took careful aim, fired, and then all three went to examine the target. Even Nasir Ali was impressed. There was a white chip in the center of the stone. It was clear that this boy was a natural marksman —clear, too, that the rifle was good.

"Now I shall have to clean the barrel again," Nasir Ali grumbled. He took the weapon from Temba and stalked on ahead toward his workshop. By the time the

Hindu and the hill boy stepped into it, the good rifle bolt had been replaced by the one with a broken firing pin. Handing over the rifle, Nasir Ali said, "Mind you, look after it. If there is so much as a scratch on it when you bring it back I shall ask compensation. Is that understood?"

"It is understood," Temba agreed. "Know this, Gunsmith," he added soberly, "when my father can walk, he will pay you for repairing the Lee-Enfield. We hillmen do not like to borrow, and you will not be sorry to have helped keep Shainu Droma alive."

Nasir Ali turned away to hide a wolfish grin. Earlier he had been cursing this year as being filled with ill luck. Perhaps he had been wrong. Allah had sent him this chicken to pluck, and in addition to the spoils they would take from the hillman and his son, there was the snow leopard and her kittens. They would make a prize worth having.

Even before the Hindu and Temba had been swallowed up by the teeming throng crowding the single street of Rakfazar Bazaar, the big, rawboned Nasir Ali was wondering if there might even be a way of cheating the Hindu of his share of the spoils. Extinguishing his forge fire, he packed and locked up his tools. Rolling some food in a blanket, he slipped a dozen cartridges into his belt and picked up his rifle. According to the plan, he was to follow the Hindu and the hill boy up the pass, keeping out of sight until darkness shrouded the hills. If all went well, darkness would bring an unpleasant surprise for Temba Droma.

8
Duel in the Hills

TEMBA AND THE HINDU LEFT RAKFAZAR BAZAAR JUST
before noon. The hill boy carried the borrowed rifle
slung over his left shoulder and led the pony, which carried a bag of fodder, the medical supplies, some food
and firewood, and a small bundle containing cooking
pots.

Temba moved with the effortless, mile-eating stride
of the hill people. Before they had gone half a mile the
Hindu was protesting. His face was dewed with sweat
and he was puffing like someone at the end of a long
race.

"There is no need for such hurry," he panted. "You
will be tired out long before sunset at this speed."

"But, sir, we must hurry," Temba explained. "The
memsahib said that if my father's life was to be saved,
we must get to him quickly and give him the white
tablets and put the ointment on his wounds."

"But at this speed we shall only kill ourselves," the
Hindu insisted. "Remember, I am not a hill boy."

"Then you follow at your own speed," Temba suggested.

"No!" snapped the Hindu, "I will ride the pony. He is a sturdy animal and can carry me without trouble."

Temba helped him mount the pony, but the rest of the day became an increasing torture for him. With neither saddle nor bridle, he had to hold on to the pony's thick mane. To add to his discomfort, the chafing of the animal's not very clean flanks soon made him feel that every square inch of skin was being rubbed off the inside of his legs.

Nor did the journey grow easier. The track grew rougher and steeper as they climbed from the lower levels of trees and tightly packed masses of rhododendrons into the barren hills. They came to the river, its rushing water churned into a milky-white flood. Head down, and grunting under the weight of the Hindu, the pony plodded on beside it, pausing only occasionally for a breather.

There were times when the Hindu closed his eyes in anguish, sure that the pony must slip and fall, taking them both to the valley below. Several times he forced Temba to halt and fetch a kettle of water so that he could slake his growing thirst. While the hill boy scrambled down to the river below, the Hindu gently massaged the ridged skin on his legs and groaned. He had never expected anything like this when he decided to accompany Temba to the mountains.

After one of these halts he drank deeply of the water the boy had brought. Then he asked hoarsely, "Do you never tire? A boy like you should not be walking uphill at this mad speed. It is a miracle you do not fall dead with fatigue."

Temba stared at him in amazement. Then with quiet dignity he said, "I am thirteen summers, sir. I am almost a man, and hillmen never tire. We are thin, but we never tire."

The Hindu could have cursed the boy. Instead, he reminded himself that when it was all over he would have more than a pocketful of rupees; perhaps more money than he had ever had. He had not forgotten Temba's story of the lair at the foot of the cliff where the snow leopard's kittens were living, and the chance that in addition to the loot he and the gunsmith might also bring back a dead snow leopard and live kittens.

An hour before the sun began to touch the distant mountaintops the fat Hindu pleaded with Temba to stop at some suitable place and make camp for the night. Unused to riding, he was enduring agonies as the pony plodded along. He was sure the skin on the inside of his legs had been rubbed off, and he was suffering from cramp. Nor could he forget the fact that the rifle Temba carried so proudly was useless. The thought of a starving snow leopard waiting somewhere along the track for them sent shivers of fear down the Hindu's spine. Had he dared, he would have dismounted and forced Temba to halt; but there was no place to stop, the track was very narrow, with a rocky wall on his right and a steep drop to the valley on his left. Still he tried to persuade Temba that if they halted now they would be able to avoid trouble with the snow leopard. After a night's rest they would be fresher, and so would the pony.

Temba merely shook his head. He was not worrying about the snow leopard. He was worrying about Shainu Droma. They must get to him quickly to put ointment on his wounds and give him the tablets. They would get him on the pony and carry him back to Rakfazar Bazaar, and the *memsahib*. Speed could mean the difference between life and death.

Only when the sun had at last vanished behind the western horizon and the swift twilight of the mountains began to shroud the pass in darkness did the Hindu finally assert himself. They had reached a spot where even a fat man could dismount, and this he did. Wagging a finger at Temba he shouted, "Not another step. Light a fire and cook some food. If I stay on that beast another minute I shall never be able to walk again. I am sure my legs have been rubbed clean of all their flesh."

Temba stared at him, and for a moment his eyes twinkled. With a sly little grin twitching his lips, he said, "Sir, surely that cannot be. There is a great deal of flesh to be worn away before it is all gone, for you are indeed a man of great fat legs."

Had there not been so much at stake, the Hindu would have struck the boy. With a great effort he stifled the flood of abuse that leaped to his tongue. His revenge would come later. It would be painfully earned, but he was sure the loot would be worth the effort. To Temba he said sadly, "Is this all the thanks you give me for my kindness? Have you forgotten that if I had not decided to help you, I could now be comfortably eating my evening meal in the peace of my own house?"

Temba had not thought of that, and was immediately sorry for poking fun at the Hindu. Apologetically he said, "You have been very kind, sir. I will fetch a kettle of water; then we can eat." He grabbed the kettle and bounded down the steep slope at a speed that made the Hindu's heart leap to his throat. The young fool seemed to think he was a mountain goat! It would be disastrous if the boy was injured at this stage.

Hardly panting, Temba returned a few minutes later with a kettle filled with ice-cold water. He lighted a small fire and cooked a stew of goat meat and barley. The Hindu pulled a wry face at his first mouthful of meat. It was not only tough and stringy, but high tasting. He would have preferred a heap of snowy rice and tender mutton, yet eat he must. He tried to console himself with the thought that within forty-eight hours he would be back in Rakfazar Bazaar with his share of the loot, able to eat what he liked, and as much as he liked.

Earlier that afternoon, in an effort to take his mind off his discomfort, the Hindu had questioned Temba about the animals and the merchandise that had been left in the compound with Shainu Droma. His eyes had gleamed as the boy innocently listed the things in the caravan packs—bales of wool, yaks' tails, blocks of red *lac*, and borax. And if they managed to shoot the snow leopard, the Hindu reflected, that, too, would bring a handsome price, for the skin of a snow leopard always found a ready buyer.

When they had finished eating, Temba began to load their small store of equipment back onto the pony. In alarm the Hindu asked, "What are you doing that for? The pony must be allowed to rest. If you——"

"He can rest later," Temba said quietly. "Surely, sir, you did not think we would stay here! Think of my father. He may be dying."

"Think of me," was the indignant retort. "I am much too sore and weary to move another yard. We stay *here*! I insist."

To the Hindu's surprise and dismay Temba did not even pause in the task of packing the stores on the pony. Shaking his head, he murmured, "We *must* go on! At least *I* must. If you wish to stay, then I will go on alone. I must reach my father this night. I have a feeling that he needs me very much."

"But you can't possibly go on in the dark," the Hindu protested. "You told me earlier that the track up the pass gets worse the higher you go. It has been bad enough even by daylight. Now that it is dark you couldn't hope to see the way."

"There will be a moon, sir," Temba assured him, and paused to point toward the hills. They were visible as a darker mass against a blue-black but star-studded sky. At one point there was a suggestion of light where the moon was coming up.

The Hindu sat back and drew so hard on his cigarette that the end glowed bright enough to light up his fat, worried face. He felt that he could not go on, yet he dared not stay here alone. After a few minutes, as the mountaintops began to show up against the rising moon, he made a last desperate attempt to force Temba to change his mind.

"Listen, boy, I am not going on," he said harshly, "and the rifle stays with me. If you remember, I promised the gunsmith that the rifle would not be allowed out of my sight, and I am a man of my word. So we stay here. I stay, and the rifle stays."

In that instant Temba knew that the man was frightened. His words were brave enough, but he spoke too loudly. There was a short pause while the hill boy and the Hindu looked at each other in the poor light of the dying fire.

"Then I shall go without the rifle, sir," Temba said. He waited a moment then, for he really did not want to go without the rifle. But when there was no reply, he added, "Keep the fire burning as long as you can. There are black bears in the hills, and at this time of the year they usually have a cub, sometimes two, so they are always hungry. Black bears can be worse than snow leopards."

"Black bears!" The Hindu scrambled stiffly to his feet, looking around fearfully.

"You are safe for the moment, sir," Temba assured him. "You have the fire and you have the rifle. It is a pity there is not more wood, for then you could have kept a bright fire all night. Bears do not like fires. However, you have the rifle."

The Hindu choked back the curses that came to his lips. *He had the rifle!* Yes, but with the firing pin broken he could only use it as a club, and who would tackle a hungry black bear with a club?

"I shall come with you," he said sulkily, "but I tell you this, I shall never befriend anyone again. This has been a lesson to me. I make great sacrifices to help a boy who is a stranger to me, and in return I get nothing but selfish ingratitude. You forget that I am not a hill-man. Are you trying to kill me by refusing to rest?"

Temba was half sorry for, half scornful of the Hindu, but he was glad the man was going on with him. They might need the rifle. He had not been lying about the black bears, though there was more chance of an attack from the injured snow leopard than from a bear.

He helped the leg-sore Hindu onto the pony, took the halter, and moved off. By this time the rim of the moon was peeping over the snow-clad mountains and bathing the valley in a pale, mysterious light. For the Hindu it was a terrifying journey. The track was narrow and rough, and though the pony was surefooted, he did occasionally stumble on a loose stone. He always recovered, but for a man with neither saddle nor reins it was frightening.

Half an hour later, when even Temba was beginning to tire, the pony suddenly threw up its head, pricked its ears, and stopped dead in its tracks.

"Why has the pony stopped?" The Hindu was thinking of black bears, and his heart began to thump.

"Quiet, sir, quiet," Temba pleaded. "The pony has heard something. I thought I did too." He grabbed at the halter rope when, as if satisfied that all was well, the pony made as if to move on again. But for some seconds the boy and the man listened intently. Then on the still air, faint yet unmistakable, came the clamor of sheep and goats. Even the Hindu heard it and asked, "What is that?"

"Our sheep and goats," Temba said, his voice rising to a sudden screech of alarm and excitement. "We are very near my father's camp and something is happening. No flock makes a noise in the night unless there is danger. Dismount. I must have the pony."

In his anxiety and excitement Temba dragged the Hindu from his seat. The Hindu was far too heavy for him to hold, so he was forced to let him slide to the ground. He hit it with a thump, but before he could protest, Temba had mounted, dug his heels into the pony's ribs, and stirred that tired animal into a trot.

The moon was well up now, and the light was good. Even so, it was dangerous for anyone to ride a pony on the rough track at a quick pace. But Temba ignored the danger and kicked his heels into the pony's ribs with such vigor that it broke into a canter.

When the Hindu realized he was alone he wailed in sudden terror. Forgetful of his aches and pains, he scrambled to his feet, using the rifle as a stick. In a terror-filled voice he yelled after Temba, "Wait! Wait for me! *Wait*! W A I T!" His voice cracked harshly on the last appeal, and a few seconds later from across the valley came a ghostly answer, an echoing "W A I T!"

If anything had been needed to make the Hindu run, it was that echo. His whole life had been spent among crowds. This was the first time he had ever been alone on a mountainside, miles away from even a tiny village, and with a starving snow leopard in the vicinity.

"WAIT!" he screamed again. "Wait for me. WAIT FOR ME!" Then he began to run.

Temba did not hear him. The unshod hooves of the pony drummed an urgent song on the rocks and thin soil. The wind sang past the boy's ears, and his heart hammered against his ribs in a painful tattoo. That distant baaing and bleating could mean only one thing—the snow leopard. Or, if it was not the snow leopard, then some other hunter equally dangerous was either in the compound or prowling outside. It told Temba, too, that his father must be unable to deal with the intruder. The sheep and goats were like part of the Droma family. They lived so close to them that they never really panicked if the humans were awake.

Even in the moonlight Temba did not recognize where he was. They came over the mountains only once each year, and it took a number of years for a man to really know the track. So Temba did not realize how near he was to the compound until he saw firelight showing through the tangled brushwood that barred the entrance.

There was no time to stop. The tired pony plunged into the thorny mass and with a tremendous creaking and cracking slid to a stop. With neither saddle nor stirrups to help him keep his seat, Temba shot over its head. He landed on all fours and slithered almost to the edge of the compound fire.

He was badly shaken, but a frightening snarl made him scramble to his feet. About seven feet from him crouched the snow leopard, and between them lay Shainu Droma. To his right their big ram, his yellow eyes reflecting the light of the fire, stood guard over the flock of sheep and goats.

The snow leopard was startled, but defiant. In the thirty-six hours since Temba began his trek to Rakfazar Bazaar she had been prowling around the compound. During much of this time Shainu Droma was delirious and lay without realizing the danger. At other times he became conscious enough to build up the fire, make himself a kettle of strong tea, and feed his flock.

With the rising of the moon, and with starvation gnawing at her, the snow leopard found courage to climb the compound wall again. Then began a battle between her and the old ram. A cunning fighter, the ram kept the leopard from his flock. At last, in desperation, the snow leopard had turned to the silent figure by the fire, hunger forcing her to join the hateful ranks of man-eaters. She had taken Shainu by the slack of his quilted coat and was dragging him toward the wall when, with a drumming of hooves, the crash of breaking brushwood, and a startled whinny from the pony, Temba Droma came hurtling into the compound. Eyes green with hate, the snow leopard crouched down, ready to fight for her prey.

When Temba scrambled to his feet he was horrified at the sight of his father lying face down, obviously dragged to his present position by the snow leopard. Hurriedly unsheathing his big knife, Temba waved it in the air and gave a wild shriek in the hope of frightening the snow leopard away.

She did shrink back a pace, hugging the ground, but

she was just as determined as the hill boy. Through eyes narrowed to slits she glared at him, her uninjured forepaw half raised. A blow from that same paw had killed their youngest dog, had killed sheep and goats. It could kill his father or him. Yet Temba knew he must do something and do it quickly. The snow leopard's first alarm was fading. At any moment she would attack.

In frightened desperation Temba yelled again, swung his knife once more, and leaped to one side. The snow leopard's slit-eyed gaze never faltered, and now her paws took a firmer grip. She was getting ready to spring.

Temba swung his long-bladed knife again, this time in a sweeping, upward arc. The knife crashed into the fire, scattering blazing embers and sending a myriad of fat sparks shooting into the air. Two of them, like fireflies, swept into the snow leopard's face. One just missed her right eye and burned for a moment in the protecting fur. The other struck the sensitive tip of her nose, like the sting of a vengeful hornet. As she lifted her good forepaw to her nose, her injured forepaw came down on a sharp stone. A lightning-sharp stab of agony shot up her muscles to the shoulder.

Temba yelled again and sent more blazing embers and more sparks shooting out toward the snow leopard. Starving though she was, this was more than she could bear. She wheeled painfully around, scrambled to the wall, and somehow got onto it and over.

The moment the animal was gone Temba wheeled and dropped to one knee by his father's side. The nagging fears that had seldom been out of his mind from the

moment he began his journey to Rakfazar Bazaar returned in a huge flood. His father was dead! The terrible
thing he had been afraid of had happened! Shainu
Droma was dead, and now he, Temba, was alone.

Grabbing the man by the shoulders he shook him,
shouting, "Father . . . FATHER! Answer! Are you all
right? Speak to me! *Father*. FATHER!" He was half
crazed with anxiety.

When there was no reply from the limp figure Temba
turned to the dying fire. Heedless of the pain, he scraped
the dying embers together and swung his cap over them
with such a fury that the cooling ashes turned to a
brighter pink. A minute or so of fanning brought flames,
which Temba fed with small twigs, then with larger
pieces of wood. Every few moments he looked anxiously
toward the wall, half afraid the snow leopard would
return.

Temba was so horrified at the thought that his father
was dead that he was suddenly afraid to touch him.
When the new twigs began to crackle and flame he
clapped his cap back on his head and turned again to
plead, "Father, do you not hear me? Speak to me! I am
Temba, your son. Do you not hear? It is Temba . . .
TEMBA, YOUR SON!"

Hardly realizing it, he was shouting loudly, and to his
joy the loudness of his plea was rewarded. Somehow the
sound penetrated the mists clouding Shainu Droma's
mind. His eyes remained closed, but his lips began to
move.

"Father!" Temba shrieked with relief. He shot a quick

glance at the wall to make sure the snow leopard had not returned, then bent to place an ear as close to his father's lips as possible.

Shainu Droma was speaking, but the sounds he made were a meaningless jumble. Half crazy with fear, Temba shook his father by the shoulders. That seemed to bring Shainu Droma closer to consciousness. He lifted a hand feebly toward his throat. This reminded Temba that the snow leopard had had his father in her grip and he began hastily to take off the thickly padded coat.

In the midst of this, the Hindu arrived. He was almost in a state of collapse as he forced aside the brushwood blocking the entrance. Drawing breath in long, wheezing gasps, he flopped down to a kneeling position and watched as the hill boy hurriedly examined Shainu Droma for new injuries.

"She did not hurt him," Temba shouted with relief. "The padding in the coat kept her teeth from his throat."

"She . . . you mean the snow leopard?" There was wheezing fear in the Hindu's voice. "She was here?"

"As you came in from the south she went over the opposite wall," Temba said proudly. "I frightened her off."

"Shouldn't we build up the fire?"

"Yes, I think . . ." Temba began, then thought of something even more important. "Will you build up the fire? I will go to the river to wash my hands and get water."

"To the river!" the Hindu could hardly believe his ears. "There is snow here. Why go to the river? If you leave this shelter the leopard will rip you to pieces."

Temba hesitated. He knew the danger, but even more important than danger to himself was his father's life. Hurriedly he explained, "River water is better for wounds. My father said so, soon after he was hurt. I'll take a torch. I'll hurry. Shainu Droma has a devil in his head. Listen to the foolish things he is saying." Temba's father was muttering again in his delirium.

While the Hindu mopped the sweat from his fat face, Temba went over to the lathered pony and unstrapped a pan. He also carefully untied the towel that contained the medical supplies. The small cake of soap fell to the ground. After standing the other things near the fire, Temba wrapped the soap in the towel and then lit a torch.

"Build up the fire," he ordered. "I'll take the rifle, just in case the snow leopard does meet me."

"The rifle . . ." The Hindu almost blurted out the truth, that the rifle was useless. After a pause he said rather lamely, "Yes, yes, take the rifle."

Temba put the towel and the soap in the fire-blackened kettle and hooked the kettle to his belt. Then, carrying the torch in his left hand, he picked up the rifle and left the compound. He held the torch high, and its red glare made the snow look pink as he trotted across to the top of the cliff.

Picking his way down the cliff path, Temba tried to remember all the things the *memsahib* had said he must do. First he must wash his hands, dry them, then put some of the ointment on his father's injuries. These were then to be covered with the thin pink cloth—the lint— and that must be held in place with a bandage. After that

Shainu Droma must be given the white tablets, six times throughout the length of a day and night.

Temba was so preoccupied with his thoughts that he forgot about the snow leopard's lair at the foot of the cliff. He turned left and at the water's edge he stopped and stuck the torch in the soft ground so that he could unhook the kettle from his belt. But obeying the unwritten law of the hill people never to be without a weapon, he kept his rifle in his right hand. He took the soap and towel out of the kettle and was filling it with water when he heard a snarl behind him.

He dropped the kettle and swung around. Holding his torch high, he saw its red light reflected in the eyes of the snow leopard. She was standing in the mouth of her lair, her fangs bared in a snarl of rage. Temba replaced his torch in the soft ground at the water's edge and lifted his rifle. The snow leopard sank, belly to the ground. Not more than four yards separated them, and at such close range Temba knew he could not miss. He squeezed gently on the trigger, took first pressure, and fired.

9
Nasir Ali

UP AT THE COMPOUND THE HINDU HAD THE WORST fright of his life less than two minutes after Temba had left to wash his hands and fetch a kettle of water. He was building up the fire with twigs when without warning a powerful hand covered his face and pulled his head back while a knee was driven, not too hard, into his back between his shoulder blades. The Hindu almost fainted from terror. Then a moment later, when the hand was removed and the knee was taken from his back, he screamed in rage as Nasir Ali laughed uproariously.

"*Aie, aie,* what a man you are!" the gunsmith chuckled. "I could have slit your throat as easy as a beggar lifts his hands for alms."

"You fool!" The Hindu was shaking with fear, and for almost a minute could say nothing more. Only when Nasir Ali began to light a cigarette did the Hindu somehow come back to life. "What are you doing here?" he demanded furiously. "The boy has gone for water and if he comes back and sees . . ."

"I saw him go. The moonlight was made for eyes like mine," Nasir Ali boasted. "I heard him talking. I followed you up the pass from the time you left Rakfazar Bazaar. Time and time again I could have killed you both with my good rifle if I had wanted, and——"

"Killing! Killing! What are you talking about, you madman?" the Hindu demanded, his face wet with the sweat of fear. "You know what the plan is. You should not have come here until the boy was asleep."

"Try and act like a man instead of a frightened boy," Nasir Ali sneered. "In my young days when we raided in the Khyber Pass we shot from the shadows, then rushed the camp and were away with the loot before anyone could do a thing. We could do the same here. Why bother with a plan?"

"If I am a frightened boy, you are a witless fool," was the bitterly sarcastic retort. "Yes, we could take these things; we could murder the boy . . . and within a week every hillman in Rakfazar Bazaar would know of it."

"How?"

"The *memsahib*," the Hindu sneered. "I told her I might come with the boy. She has a long memory. We stick to our plan . . . and then there is blame for neither of us. Now go, and don't come back until the moment is ripe."

Nasir Ali rose.

"See that there is some food cooking," he growled sulkily. "I have eaten nothing since noon. I'll come over there, where the big flat stone is on the wall top," and he pointed to the place. "And don't ask why. *I'll* tell *you*. This hill boy will push the brushwood back in place when he returns. Hill people are born with sense; not like some people I know." With a sneering laugh Nasir Ali turned and, rifle in hand, swaggered out of the compound, leaving the Hindu muttering things he would have liked to have said out loud to the gunsmith but knew he would never dare.

Spluttering with anger, he filled a cooking pot with snow from a corner of the compound, then put in some of the goat meat they had brought with them from Rakfazar Bazaar. He had just satisfied himself that the fire was burning as brightly as possible when Temba returned.

"I heard you coming," the Hindu lied, watching Temba do exactly as Nasir Ali had said he would do— push the brushwood into the opening in the compound wall. "You didn't see the snow leopard?"

For a moment Temba hesitated. Then he said soberly, "I saw her, and I thought to kill her. She was as near to me as the brushwood is."

The Hindu gulped. Thinking of the rifle that would not fire, he was suddenly dry-throated. What had happened? Did the boy know the rifle was useless? With an effort he asked, "Why do you say you 'thought to kill her'?"

"I had a bad cartridge," Temba said soberly. "She was about to spring as I squeezed the trigger, but there was only a click."

"And . . . what . . ." This was all the Hindu could manage to say.

"The click must have startled her, for she rushed back into her cave. I grabbed my things and ran. I have not even washed my hands. That snow leopard has a devil looking after her. My father has fired at her and missed. Then, when I could not have missed, the gun didn't fire."

"Never mind, you will get another chance. As for washing your hands, I know something of this. You can do it with snow. Bring a big handful and I will show you."

He showed Temba how to wet his hands with snow melting before the fire, how to rub soap on his skin, then work up a lather. The towel was dirty after Temba had dried his hands, but the hill boy was satisfied. He had done what the *memsahib* had ordered. His hands were cleaner than they had been, though they were far from being spotless.

The fire was stirred to a brighter glow, and in that light Temba took off the rags wrapped about his father's injured leg. He cleansed the wounds and it must have been painful, for Shainu Droma groaned, and then opened his eyes.

"What I am going to do, Father, will make your leg well," Temba assured him. "I spoke to the *memsahib* in Rakfazar Bazaar, and she has given me medicine and something to make your leg as good as it ever was. Lie still, and afterward there will be hot tea and goat meat."

Shainu Droma closed his eyes again, and Temba began his doctoring. He spread penicillin ointment over the claw wounds, covered them with lint, and wrapped a bandage over the lint. It was not a very neat piece of bandaging, but it would hold the lint in place and keep out air and dirt. When he finished, he forced his father to sit up.

Shainu Droma's eyes were open, but he did not seem to be seeing anything. Nevertheless, when Temba pushed two of the antibiotic tablets into his mouth, Shainu swallowed them, and even gulped thirstily at the water Temba offered him. The ice-cold snow water brought a flicker of life to his eyes, and he even managed a tired little smile as Temba was laying him down again.

"He will live," Temba prophesied. "He knew me."

The Hindu ladled out soup, and he and Temba ate a meal of the goat meat. It was their second dinner that evening but they were hungry. Temba made a kettle of strong tea, and when that was finished the Hindu said coaxingly, "Now, boy, lie down and sleep. I shall keep watch in case that spotted *shaitan* comes back." And picking up the useless rifle he pushed the safety catch to the "off" position. To impress Temba with his wakefulness, he lighted a cigarette and, with the rifle across his knees, puffed in apparent content.

The fire was burning brightly, and since there was nothing more he could do, Temba wrapped himself in his homespun blanket and lay down. The ground was hard, for less than an inch of soil covered the solid rock, but this was a familiar bed to Temba. Believing the Hindu to be his friend, he was soon asleep.

The Hindu puffed at his cigarette and watched. He saw the tired eyes close, noted the steady rise and fall of the hill boy's chest. He was asleep; the boy's father was either asleep or unconscious, and somewhere outside the compound Nasir Ali was waiting for the agreed signal.

Standing and lifting his hand, the Hindu waved the glowing tip of his cigarette from side to side.

Within twenty seconds first Nasir Ali's turban and then his eyes were visible. Then, when he realized that the hill boy and his father were both lying motionless, he heaved himself up onto the flat stone. The Hindu had already picked up the stone he had searched for and found earlier. It was round and fitted his hand perfectly. With one blow from it he could knock out Temba when the boy sat up. Once again he waved to Nasir Ali, then nerved himself for his part in the attack.

For a moment the gunsmith squatted on the wall top. Red, dancing shafts of light from the fire played across his big form, lighted up his hawklike features, and seemed to put sparks in his gleaming eyes. Poised for a leap, his rifle in both hands, he presented a terrifying figure. As he leaped, he squeezed the trigger of the rifle, and the quiet of the night was shattered by the loud bang that a black-powder cartridge makes. At the same time Nasir Ali gave a bull-throated roar: "Bandits! Bandits!"

This was all part of the scheme to shake Temba to a terrified wakefulness, so panic-stricken that he would not know what was happening and would hardly remember afterward what hit him. This was the moment when the Hindu was to bring his stone down with a thump on the back of the hill boy's head.

The attack began and ended in less than twenty seconds. As Nasir Ali landed in the compound the sheep and goats came to sudden, frenzied life. Temba, born to a life of hardship and danger, could drop off to sleep as quickly as any wild animal and waken just as quickly. Like a wild animal, too, he woke in full possession of his senses. At the thunderous roar of the rifle and the bellow from Nasir Ali, Temba rolled away from the fire, threw off his blanket, and got to one knee. This moved him out of the Hindu's reach, even if that man had been alert enough to use his stone.

Amid the pandemonium of baas and bleats, the tethered pony whirled around, and as his head went down his hind feet came up. It was a thunderbolt kick.

Luckily for Nasir Ali the pony's hooves were unshod. The blow caught the gunsmith on the right hip and the lower ribs. There was a *thud* and, big man though he was, the impact lifted him off his feet and pitched him to one side as if he were no heavier than a bag of feathers. Sheep and goats leaped in all directions. One stumbled across Nasir Ali and flopped on his head.

Temba's ears were still ringing with the shouted "Bandits! Bandits!" and his mind was filled with the one thing to do when a camp was attacked—begin shooting. Temba leaped across to pick up Nasir Ali's rifle, which had bounced to the ground when the pony's hooves took him in the ribs. The Hindu, now on his feet, made a half-hearted swing at the hill boy with his heavy stone—and missed.

Unaware of this, Temba grabbed the rifle. The gun-smith was making a feeble attempt to rise. Since there wasn't time to reload, Temba cracked this intruder smartly across the head with the butt of the gun. Nasir Ali flopped face down and lay still. Only his thick turban saved him from a crushed skull. Temba did not give him a second glance. Expecting more bandits to storm the compound wall, he pivoted like a top and came face to face with the Hindu, who was nerving himself to try again for a knockout blow.

"Get our rifle," Temba yelled, not for a moment imagining that the stone the Hindu held was intended for him. Now he worked the bolt of Nasir Ali's weapon, ejected the spent cartridge case and, dropping a hand to his own pouch, loaded another round in its place. A quick glance around the compound walls satisfied him no one was in sight, but he knew the danger of a sniper's shot fired through some crevice. With a well-aimed kick he stirred the fire to greater life, sending a thousand sparks dancing like fireflies into the night.

The Hindu stood like a man suddenly paralyzed. When Temba yelled for him to pick up their rifle he obeyed like a mechanical doll. Eyes bulging, he watched Temba, quick and nervous as a cat, swiveling around and around, waiting for the shots that might come at any moment from the rest of the bandits he thought must be moving about outside the walls.

The sheep and goats were packed into a heaving mass in one part of the compound. The pony, frightened by the yelling and the shot, snorted and plunged wildly, threatening to break its halter rope any second. Temba screamed at the Hindu to secure the pony, and again was obeyed without a word. Flustered and trembling, the fat man grabbed the halter rope and tried to calm the pony with frantic pleas. "Quiet . . . be still. Come on, now, be quiet. Be quiet." Inwardly he was shaking; sweat dappled his face. He was terrified lest Nasir Ali blurt out the truth when he regained consciousness. He very well knew that hill people had no policemen to keep law and order but punished wrongdoers in their own way. If the truth came out, the punishment would be a brutal beating—or it could be death.

"Shall I tie this one's hands?" the Hindu asked, when Temba seemed to begin to be less worried. Since there had been no sign from the bandits Temba thought had attacked, after that first shot and shout, he was beginning to wonder if there were more than one.

Grabbing a piece of rope from one of the packs of merchandise, the Hindu began to tie Nasir Ali's wrists together. At that, the gunsmith opened his eyes. Recognizing the Hindu, he asked, "What happened? Did you knock the boy——" and that was as far as he was allowed to go. Terrified lest Temba should come over and guess that he and Nasir Ali were partners, the Hindu ripped off the gunsmith's turban and hurriedly stuffed one end in his mouth, effectively gagging him.

The treatment shocked Nasir Ali. He had taken a nasty kick from the pony and Temba's hard head blow from his own rifle, but he was tough, and he began to try to get to his feet. Then, after a podgy knee was driven into his stomach, he was turned face down and his wrists tied behind his back. Gasping, he still tried to rise, but the Hindu knelt on him and whispered fiercely, "Lie still, you fool. The boy has your rifle, and if he thinks you are about to get free he'll shoot. Lie still. I'll free you later."

At first Nasir Ali gritted his teeth in pain and rage, but then he relaxed and even allowed his ankles to be tied. The Hindu was thinking hard. One thing he had to do—and that was convince Temba he had no idea Nasir Ali would attack the camp. Looking up, he called, "Boy, boy, come here, quick! Maybe there are no others outside. I've just got a good look at this fellow. He is the gunsmith from Rakfazar Bazaar, Nasir Ali."

Temba, still fearing another attack, had never ceased circling the compound. Now he stopped in amazement. More than once he had been in camp with his father when bandits had attacked them. They had always been poor, desperate men, willing to risk their lives for a handful of rupees, or the chance of stealing a few sheep or goats. It seemed impossible to him that a gunsmith should become a bandit. The hill people looked on gunsmiths as skilled craftsmen, perhaps not rich, but certainly not poor enough to turn bandit.

Still careful not to make himself an easy target, he scurried across the compound to the Hindu, who was standing over his prisoner. Hoping to convince the boy that he was no friend of the trussed-up man, the Hindu kicked Nasir Ali in the ribs and shouted, "Who else is with you? How many others are there?" He bent low as Nasir Ali rolled his eyes angrily. Speech was impossible, for the turban that the Hindu used to gag him had been pulled so tight that his jaws were quite immovable.

When there was no reply, Nasir Ali was kicked again, and again asked for an answer. Then Temba said angrily, "How can the man speak when his turban chokes him? Take the rag from his mouth; then he will speak." He dropped the muzzle of his rifle onto Nasir Ali's ribs and said harshly, "Speak quickly, and remember I have my finger hard on the trigger. If your friends shoot, you die too."

The Hindu was already on one knee, fumbling with the gag and praying silently that Nasir Ali would get his message and cooperate. Yet he was sweating with fear when he finally drew the gag away. If Nasir Ali had not understood his silent appeal, and should denounce him as a double-crosser, a bullet from the rifle Temba held might finish the whole thing.

Luckily for the Hindu, Nasir Ali had also realized the danger. The fury faded from his eyes and to the Hindu's amazement and relief he croaked an apology and a plea for mercy. "O, brave hill boy, be merciful. I am a poor gunsmith. For a number of seasons now life has been hard and it has grown ever harder. I am sorry for coming here. I was suddenly afraid that the rifle I lent you might not be returned. That is why I followed you."

The hill boy looked up questioningly at the Hindu, but his eyes were closed in a surge of great thankfulness. Then, suddenly aware that the hill boy was staring at him, the Hindu threatened the man at his feet with an angry, "How many came with you, murdering dog? Speak, or your throat will be cut at once. How many?" And he kicked Nasir Ali with the toe of his sandal.

Again the gunsmith swallowed the anger that boiled in him. "Sir, I came alone," he said meekly. "This is true, and I swear it by the Prophet. May I burn forever in the pit of Gehenna if I am not telling the truth."

"We'll have you by a smaller fire where we can see you better," Temba said coldly, "and I promise you, if there is an attack by your friends, be sure you will die at once. You understand?"

"I understand," Nasir Ali said eagerly. He was furious

at being spoken to thus by a boy on whose chin even soft down had not yet begun to grow, but he managed to sound both apologetic and humble. "Keep the rifle muzzle pressed against my heart, O hillman, for I know that no other attack will be made. I came here completely alone."

Nasir Ali was dragged unceremoniously closer to the fire, and after Temba had checked the ropes that bound his wrists and ankles, the hill boy and the Hindu sat down. The sheep and goats were quieter now, and even the pony was standing with his head bowed, as if preparing for sleep. Hopefully, the Hindu suggested that he would keep watch while Temba lay down again. His answer was a curt "No." With Nasir Ali's rifle across his knees Temba sat and stared into the fire. Now and again his head nodded from utter weariness, but his eyes never closed completely.

During all this commotion Shainu Droma had lain quietly. An hour before dawn Temba woke his father and forced him to swallow two more of the antibiotic tablets. He did not know whether or not Shainu Droma's temperature was going down, but the *memsahib* had said two tablets six times a day, and Temba had decided that if he gave them to his father three times in the night and then at dawn, noon, and sunset, that would divide the day up fairly well.

Like Temba, the Hindu did not sleep. He was tormenting his brain for some way out of this unexpected situation. He hardly dared think what Nasir Ali would say and do if, or when, he was released. Unless the Hindu could get hold of the rifle now lying across Temba's knees, they were in deep trouble. The rifle he had was useless, for it was the one that had a bolt with a broken firing pin.

The Hindu kept stealing glances at the hill boy. He reflected that when he first met Temba he had seen him merely as a simple boy from the high hills. He *was* only a boy, but in the past thirty-six hours something seemed to have happened to him. He had shouldered the responsibilities of getting help for his father and met all difficulties with the coolness and the determination of someone twice his age.

Nasir Ali, too, sat deep in thought. During the first cold hour before sunrise he watched Temba make a meal of strong tea into which barley meal and a nob of butter had been tossed. It was all the breakfast they were to get, and even the Hindu was glad of a second mug of the brew. He gulped it down, shivering inwardly, yet too hungry to refuse it. Then he sat staring into space and trying to think of a way to outwit Temba and set Nasir Ali free.

It was near midmorning when Shainu Droma opened his eyes and asked for food. Temba, delighted to hear his father speak sensibly, gave him some goat-meat stew. Shainu was very weak and drifted off to sleep almost immediately after he had eaten. Temba felt his father's forehead to see if the fire was leaving him. Excitedly, the hill boy spoke to the Hindu. "Sir, I just felt my father's head. The fire devil must be leaving his blood. Feel! Do you not think his skin is cooler? We will get him on the pony, and by sunset we could——"

"Kill him!" was the tart retort. "Boy, have you no sense

at all? How can we take a man so weak down a steep mountain track? He is too ill to sit on a beast as unsteady as this accursed pony. Keep him sleeping for another day and by then he will be himself again."

"The *memsahib* said to hurry!" Temba insisted.

"The *memsahib* has never ridden a pony on this mountain track," the Hindu said feelingly. "Even I, much traveled though I am, ache in every bone, and I am not a sick man."

"But the sheep and the goats," Temba insisted, "how are they to eat? We have only one small bale of hay left. It is not enough for them. See how they scrape the ground in the hope of finding a blade of grass."

"You could take them outside, two or three at a time," the Hindu suggested, for Temba had given him an idea. "You have a rifle, and if that snow leopard does appear, you could shoot her. I will stay here and keep the fire burning and keep watch over your father, the prisoner, and the rest of the flock."

Temba would not agree. The *memsahib* had insisted that Shainu Droma must be taken down to Rakfazar Bazaar as soon as possible, so that she could help heal his injured leg. Brushing aside the Hindu's suggestion, he · insisted they get his father onto the pony.

Agreeing, the Hindu tugged when Temba pulled. Shainu Droma was a heavy man and quite unable to help himself. So for almost ten minutes the hill boy and the Hindu struggled, one to get the injured man on the pony, the other to prevent him from being placed there.

When Shainu Droma was finally on the pony's back, the Hindu managed to give a sly pull on his shoulders, and a moment later the injured man had slid to the ground again.

Exhausted with the struggle, Temba agreed then that it was impossible to start out that day. Wearily he moved the brushwood aside and allowed four of the clamoring sheep and goats out to graze. While they pawed at the thin snow, searching for new grass, he watched and tried not to go to sleep. All but four animals had grazed when the tragedy occurred. Eyes heavy as lead, Temba sank to his haunches and dozed. Within five minutes a sheep and a goat were killed.

The snow leopard had watched unseen almost from the first moment Temba had brought the animals out into the open. She looked even leaner now than two days earlier. Her kittens were growing and demanding more and more milk, draining her strength away. Crouched behind a rock, she was quivering with expectancy, yet afraid to come out because of Temba. Two hours passed. When Temba dropped to a squatting position and his eyes closed, she got her chance. As if drawn by a magnet, a sheep and a goat strayed nearer and nearer to her hiding place behind a rock. She had chosen her spot well, for a light breeze was blowing from them to her and they did not get her scent. Heads down, cropping busily at the thin grass, the goat and sheep drew within easy range.

Despite her injured forepaw, the snow leopard managed a clean, majestic leap. The killing was quick and painless. Only the doomed goat managed a bleat of alarm.

Temba, dozing one moment was on his feet the next. Before the snow leopard had time to grab either of her victims the roar of his rifle shattered the peace, and the bullet ricocheted from a rock so close that it threw stone dust into the hunter's face.

With a startled screech, the snow leopard sank down. Temba hurriedly ejected the spent cartridge, rammed another into the breech, and fired again. But he was tired. The second bullet went even wider than the first, and the spotted hunter limped away, slithering down the cliff path before a third shot could be fired.

The startled Hindu came hurrying out to see what was happening and helped carry the two dead animals back to the compound. There were still four of the depleted flock that had not yet tasted grass. Temba, feeling very dejected, decided to take them out two at a time and on a rope lead. If the snow leopard tried again, she would have to come within point-blank range. Temba suggested the Hindu might try shooting the animal, but got an emphatic though apologetic answer. "I am no marksman. The only way I could kill an animal would be to put the muzzle against its head." Then the Hindu made a suggestion. "There is another way out of this difficulty. Why wait for this accursed leopard to do the hunting? Why not hunt her?"

Temba thought for a moment, then shook his head. He was angry and distressed at losing two more of his animals, but the important thing was to get through the night safely. When morning came they would start down the pass for Rakfazar Bazaar. Refusing to listen to the Hindu's suggestion, he cautiously led two more of his flock out to graze.

10
More
Schemes

BACK IN THE COMPOUND NASIR ALI SAT UP. THE HINDU
had removed his bonds the moment Temba took the first
of the sheep and goats out to graze. Even so, the gunsmith's ankles and wrists were still stinging painfully as
blood flowed back into his feet and hands. The ropes had
been tied tightly.

"I have a fresh idea," the Hindu said, lighting a cigarette.

"Never mind ideas," Nasir Ali snarled. "Give me that
knife, and when the boy returns I'll slit his throat. If we
get rid of him, everything———"

"If you keep talking like that I'll slit your throat!" The
Hindu, usually so soft-voiced and meek, suddenly lost
his temper. Snatching up the rifle, he swung it by the
barrel so that the butt was poised over the gunsmith's
head. It was so unexpected that Nasir Ali was momentarily petrified. He was at a disadvantage, for the strength
had not yet returned to his feet. He knew, for he had
tried to walk a little earlier and had fallen.

"I am sorry." The Hindu lowered the rifle, almost frightened at his own unexpected fury. "But you *must* listen to me," he went on. "If you follow my plan you will be on your way to Rakfazar Bazaar before the moon is up and will be taking with you everything of value in the camp."

"*I* will take everything?" Nasir Ali said sarcastically. "You are too generous! And what will *you* be taking? When you talk about *me* taking things of value I know you are planning to cheat me. You don't give anything away. You are a——"

"I am going to persuade the boy to sit up in a tree to shoot the leopard," the Hindu interrupted, ignoring the gunsmith's insults. Then, as a precaution, he helped Nasir Ali move a little farther away from Shainu Droma. The hillman appeared to be sleeping, but the Hindu could not afford to risk being overheard. "I will persuade the boy to sit up in a tree platform as the British used to do when seeking to kill a man-eating tiger," he whispered to Nasir Ali. "As you probably know, they used to stake a bullock below the tree to draw the tiger near. We will tie a goat to lure this *shaitan* of a snow leopard."

"Go on, I listen with aching ears," Nasir Ali sneered.

"The leopard will come," the Hindu said, smiling a little nervously now. "She is starving or she would never come out in the sunlight."

"Interesting," Nasir Ali scoffed. "No doubt you will soon come to the part for me to play. Is there a part?"

"There is," the Hindu said stiffly, annoyed at Nasir Ali's sarcasm. "While the boy is sitting in the tree, I shall be helping you pack pannier loads on the pony. Before the boy gets back, whether or not the leopard appears, you will be leading the pony down the track to Rakfazar Bazaar."

He paused and waited. Nasir Ali, his eyes puckered, stared at him but said nothing.

"Don't you think it is a good idea?" the Hindu asked anxiously. "There is no bloodshed, and we get everything."

"What a fool you are!" Nasir Ali snorted contemptuously. "We take the hillman's trade goods and what do you think the boy will do then? He may be only a boy, but he acts like a man." Nasir Ali lifted his hand to the lump on his head; it would be tender for days, for Temba had wielded the rifle butt with plenty of energy.

"I have thought of the boy," was the quiet retort, and now the Hindu's eyes were alight with glee. "I shall stay here. When he returns, perhaps with the dead leopard, he will find me lying here, apparently unconscious. When he revives me I shall tell him you managed to get free, attacked me, then took the pony and all the goods. Wait . . . wait," he pleaded as Nasir Ali seemed about to explode. "I have more to say."

"And *I* am pleased to know it," was the stinging retort. "Do you think that I am soft in the head? I do the stealing; I do the attacking. I have already attacked the camp and been beaten over the head by this hill boy, to say nothing of having half my ribs cracked by the accursed pony. Now I am to take the blame for the theft, while you return to Rakfazar Bazaar as the good, kindly

Hindu who helped the hill family. You must think I am completely mad."

"I *am* a man who thinks," the Hindu said stiffly. "You are forgetting that if you take the pony it will be impossible for the boy to get his father down the pass. Do you imagine he will leave him in order to follow you to Rakfazar Bazaar? He will not. Nor will there be any way to move his father once the pony is gone. Then I shall offer to hurry down to Rakfazar Bazaar, give the alarm, and buy another pony."

"Yes, go on." There was still no friendliness in Nasir Ali's voice.

"I shall not raise the alarm, of course," the Hindu pointed out. "I shall not even enter the village. I shall join you at a place we shall name. The goods will be sold, including the pony, and by the time this boy Temba realizes I am not returning with help, we shall be far away. We will be at least two, if not three, days ahead of him, and who can find us after three days? Now what do you say? Is it good, or have you a better plan?"

Nasir Ali sat rubbing his aching wrists. He was glowering, but at last he looked up. "This plan had better work," he said angrily, "if it doesn't, then I'll slit this hill boy's throat, and perhaps yours as well."

It was time for Temba's return. Nasir Ali eased himself back to where he had been before, and snarled as the Hindu advanced with the wrist and ankle ropes, "And don't knot them this time. They are to be just looped around."

"Of course, of course. Quick! The boy may be back any minute. He's worried, very worried."

"So would anybody be, dealing with you," Nasir Ali growled. He rewound the rope loosely around his ankles before sulkily holding out his wrists. This time the Hindu wrapped the wrist bonds loosely and there was no knot.

The Hindu spent the next several minutes examining and gloating over the various packs of merchandise. At the same time he kept an eye on the fire and occasionally looked at the sleeping Shainu Droma. When Temba returned with the two animals he had been grazing, they were still bleating hungrily. They had been conscious all the time that the snow leopard was watching them and had not been able to eat their fill.

"She is getting bolder," Temba said soberly. "She will come again tonight, I am sure, and our supply of firewood is very low. We must go out for more wood."

The Hindu could not have wished for a better opportunity of putting forward his scheme. He told Temba how, in the days when the British ruled India, white men hunted man-eating tigers by sitting in a tree platform with a bullock staked below. The man-eater would come for an easy meal, and be shot while killing the bullock.

"We could do this," the Hindu said coaxingly, "and finish off this accursed leopard. That would be the end of our worries."

Temba was uneasy about the scheme, but the shortage of firewood and the fact that the day was beginning to draw to a close finally made him agree.

With Temba carrying Nasir Ali's good rifle, he and the Hindu went out to look for a suitable tree. It took them some time to find it. There were not many trees, and the best one for their purpose was a good eighty yards from the compound. It was no more than fourteen feet high, but with much struggling they managed to lop off a few branches and tie them horizontally to make a crude platform on which Temba could crouch.

The Hindu tested the platform and frowned at the way it creaked and swayed. "You will have to sit very still," he cautioned.

"It will be worth it if we can kill the *shaitan*," Temba muttered. He would have climbed into his position there and then if the Hindu had not stopped him.

"Not yet. Leopards are clever, and I am sure that this one is even now watching us. First we will drive her back down the cliff. Then you can climb into the tree and I will fetch the goat. One thing you must remember— when you are in the tree you must not speak to the goat. If it knows you are in the tree it will feel quite safe and will go to sleep. If it thinks it has been left alone it will be afraid and will cry out for its companions—and that is what we want. Its bleating will bring the snow leopard and you will be able to get a close-range shot. If this accursed hunter waits until the moon comes up, so much the better. You should have no difficulty finishing her off, for you are a good shot."

They walked toward the edge of the cliff, the Hindu talking loudly, and his ruse worked. The snow leopard had been watching them intently. Alarmed by their approach, she slid away from behind the rock where she had been concealed and was gone down the cliff path before Temba could even lift his rifle.

"We cannot fail." The Hindu was bubbling with enthusiasm as they turned back toward the tree. "You get onto the platform and I will fetch the goat."

Ten minutes later he returned with a young, almost white goat. It trotted along quite happily until it was tethered to a stake they had driven into the ground just below the tree. Then, as if it knew it was to be left there alone, it began to bleat piteously.

"That is what we want," the Hindu gloated. "Keep on bleating, goat. The louder you cry the sooner the snow leopard will come to finish you off!" Laughing, he walked back to the compound.

Temba had never been quite sure in his mind about this fat Hindu. Sometimes the man seemed anxious to be friendly; at other times there was something in his manner that made the young hill boy suspicious. Now, after his jeering remark to the goat, Temba decided he did not like him at all. There was nothing new in the killing of a sheep or a goat. His family lived on such meat; but when an animal had to die the killing was quick and merciful. They had never left an animal to be attacked by a leopard.

Looking down at the goat, the hill boy suddenly hated the Hindu and was sorry for the goat. Straining at the rope, the young thing stared after the retreating white-clad figure, bleating anxiously as if pleading not to be left out there in the gathering gloom. Temba was tempted to slip down from the platform and release the animal, but he resisted the temptation. To set it free would be stupid. They had to kill the snow leopard, and the goat was one way of luring the spotted hunter within range of his rifle. Still, he did not like this way of doing things. "I'll try and kill her before she gets the goat," he promised himself.

The goat, knowing nothing of this promise, and unaware that Temba was so near, continued to bleat anxiously. Now and then it made a desperate lunge forward in an attempt to snap the rope, but all it succeeded in doing was to jerk itself back on its haunches and tighten the rope about its neck, changing its bleating into a strangled squeak.

The red glow in the west deepened, turned purple, and the last of the color in the sky drained away. Over the top of the mountains stars began to prick the rapidly deepening blue of the sky. Then, except for the pitiful crying of the goat, there was silence; the short, peaceful silence that comes to lonely places when the day has just died.

Even the goat seemed to feel the peace, for its bleating grew less, and at last it lay down. After a minute or so there came from the direction of the compound a faint baa-aaa, a reminder that the young goat's companions were quite near. The sound brought the roped goat to its feet again, and once more it began bleating. For ten minutes the anxious bleatings went on without pause. Then, quite suddenly, they stopped. Temba's pulse began to race and, holding his breath, he listened anxiously. Beneath the tree the goat was also listening, its ears cocking first this way, then that. Temba could just see the goat as a vague gray shape but he knew it had either heard something or got a scent. Heard or scented, the thing that had silenced the goat must be the snow leopard.

There was a clatter of tiny hooves as the goat, which had been straining in the direction of the compound, swung around and faced in the direction of the top of the cliff. Temba pushed the safety catch of his rifle to the "off" position and gently lifted the weapon to his shoulder. He was tingling with excitement. This time there would be no mistake. His eyes were accustomed to the gloom and, providing his rifle did not misfire, he was sure he would have no difficulty in killing the snow leopard.

11
Night of
Terror

WHILE TEMBA SAT ON THE TREE PLATFORM WAITING
for the snow leopard to appear, the Hindu had returned
to the compound. He assured Nasir Ali that everything
was proceeding according to plan. The gunsmith lighted
a cigarette and squatted on the ground, preparing to en-
joy his first real smoke in twenty-four hours, but the
Hindu insisted that they must carry out their plan immediately.

"This snow leopard is starving," he said. "She will not
wait for the moon to rise before she comes up to kill the
goat."

"And be killed herself," Nasir Ali added.

"Which only means that the hill boy will come hurrying back here," was the impatient retort. "The sooner
you are away from here, the better I shall feel. I tell you
this, Nasir Ali, I am beginning to fear that boy. He is
young, but he behaves more like a man than a boy. And
. . . what are you doing that for?" he wailed, as Nasir Ali
kicked the fire to a greater blaze.

"We need light," was the jeering reply. "You may be afraid of the boy, but you have a companion who isn't afraid of him or anyone else. All right, don't gape like a fish out of water. Let's get the things packed on the pony."

They brought the shaggy-haired pony nearer the fire so that they could see better what they were doing. Before the packages that had been carried by the sheep and goats over the high passes could be reloaded, they had to be untied and made up into bundles of six, to be slung three on each side over the pony's back. As they worked, both men were in high spirits. When these bundles, the result of a year's hard work by Shainu Droma and his family, were sold there would be far more than the two hundred rupees Nasir Ali had first been promised. It would be more like three hundred each, perhaps even more. And the snow leopard could bring them still another fifty rupees.

As they worked they could hear the distant bleating of the unhappy goat—the "bait" staked out to lure the snow leopard to her death. The anguished bleating carried easily on the night air.

"Listen to it," Nasir Ali chuckled, pausing as he tied up some bottles of musk oil. "You picked one with a good voice, friend. It is doing its best to get itself killed. Any four-legged hunters within a mile will hear that noise."

The Hindu paused for a moment to listen, and nodded agreement. He was panting, for the loads were heavy and the pony was restless. Every time the two men tried to throw their hastily made pannier packs over the animal's withers, it seemed to move in another direction.

"I don't think we'll get all the packages on this accursed beast," the Hindu gasped when they had secured three more bundles. "Do you think you could carry some? It would be a pity to leave——"

"Me—carry some of these?" Nasir Ali asked, his voice showing his utter amazement. "Do you think my mother was a camel? Listen, when you come down to Rakfazar Bazaar to buy another pony for the boy and his father you can carry some. After all you will need money to buy the pony. The boy will understand that. As for me carrying packages. *Tcha*! No man with the trade of gunsmith in his fingers becomes a pack animal. You——" and there he stopped as the Hindu dropped a warning hand on his arm.

"The goat . . ." he said, his voice quivering. "It has stopped bleating."

The gunsmith, about to brush the hand off his arm, paused and listened. Now the night seemed very still indeed. The sheep and goats in the compound were sleeping. So was Shainu Droma. The pony stood with drooping head. Everything was quiet. Nasir Ali nodded. His companion was right—the pathetic bleating had stopped. Both men were sure what the silence meant: the snow leopard had appeared and the panic-stricken goat was waiting—waiting for its death.

Taut-nerved, the Hindu listened. There was a prickling at the back of his neck as if the soft hairs there had suddenly become tiny quivering wires. His hands grew clammy as he waited for a sudden screech—perhaps a death bleat. The seconds passed; the silence grew heavier. Suddenly the Hindu could stand it no longer.

"Come on, let's finish packing," he said to Nasir Ali. "If the boy shoots the leopard he will be back here in minutes. And don't forget—he has the good rifle."

They went back to work with even more feverish haste.

Then, at last, the silence of the night was shattered by a pitiful bleat. *Ay-ay-ay-ay-ay-ay-ay!* The report of the rifle followed. The Hindu quivered and closed his eyes, but Nasir Ali, giving his companion a dig in the back with his elbow, said, "Come on, this is no time for trembling. Once he is sure the leopard is dead the boy will be back!"

The snow leopard had wasted no time after first hearing the frightened bleating of the goat. Leaving her kittens, she had hurried up the cliff path. Her damaged forepaw was beginning to heal, but she was still close to starvation and desperate enough to take any risk to make a kill.

With the wind blowing from her to the goat, she had no warning at all that a human was near. She stood for a few moments sniffing the air, but it was clean and gave no hint of danger. The terrified bleating of the goat stopped. Crouched low, she listened. She heard the clatter of tiny hooves as the goat swung around to face her. Moving forward as soundless as a shadow, she caught two sounds—the harsh breathing of the goat and the creak of the rope that tethered it.

In another ten minutes the moon would rise, and the snow leopard might then have seen the shape among the branches of the tree. But with her gnawing hunger there could be no waiting.

At a crouching run she hurried forward, not stopping until she was about eight yards from the goat. The young animal became petrified with terror. Its limbs slackened; its eyes bulged. It could see the vague shape of the snow leopard, yet the tight rope about its own neck made escape impossible.

In the tree, crouched precariously on the rickety platform, Temba was as tense as the animals. With the safety catch in the "off" position and the butt cuddled to his shoulder, he could feel its coolness against his right cheek. He had taken the first pressure on the trigger. As yet he could not see the snow leopard, though he was sure she must be very close as he had got the faint, musty smell of her. His heart was beating so loudly that he could hear its *thum-thum-thum*. His hands began to grow clammy on the rifle. He was holding his breath, waiting for the first move.

The young goat, as if realizing that the attack must come any second, suddenly shattered the silence with a pitiful *Ay-ay-ay-ay-ay-ay-ay*!

The sound was so unexpected that Temba's trigger finger tightened involuntarily. Since he had already taken the first pressure, this extra tightening of the finger was sufficient to fire the rifle.

Bang! The rifle kicked, and a yard-long flame slashed the darkness. The report of the shot was like the crack of a thunderbolt, and by the light of the gun flash Temba saw the snow leopard.

Just as the frightened bleat caused Temba to fire too soon, so it also unleashed all the power behind the snow leopard's coiled muscles. In that flame-lit second he saw her sailing through the air in a wonderful leap. She looked both magnificent and frightening. Her forepaws were at full stretch, and for a split instant the red light of the gun flash lit up her bared claws. Her mouth, opened wide, showed her gleaming fangs, and her eyes seemed to blaze with red fire.

At the foot of the tree the young goat, too, had been tense-muscled. At the thunderous roar of the gun she leaped sideways. Her second bleat of terror mingled with a snarl of surprise and furious anger from the snow leopard.

To Temba the snow leopard seemed to be leaping straight for him, as if drawn to the momentary flame from the gun. Her great leap took her to the exact spot where the young goat had been—but it was no longer there. It had jumped the full distance of the rope and was standing, head down, ready to fight for its life.

The snow leopard hit the foot of the tree, and with the savage bravery of her kind she immediately began to climb. Fear and caution were forgotten as she seemed to sense that she could never get away with the captive goat until she had dealt with this thing that roared at her and spat flame.

The very slenderness of the tree was a hindrance, for her weight caused it to sway from side to side. As she heaved upward, one paw slid off the slim bole, tearing the thin bark as if it were paper. She grunted as her chest struck the bole. Then, reaching up with her other paw, she dug her claws deep into the moss-covered wood.

The tree shook and creaked as if in the grip of an angry giant. The rickety platform on which Temba crouched seemed about to fall to pieces. In a desperate attempt to keep from being thrown to the ground, Temba grabbed at the nearest branches with both hands, dropping his precious rifle.

The snow leopard clawed higher, and reached the edge of the platform even as Temba realized that his weapon was gone. He backed away, trying to drag his long knife from its sheath. As he did so one of the platform lashings broke with a crack and at once the whole platform tilted, almost throwing the snow leopard back to the ground.

Snarling even more ferociously she clawed at the tree bark, ripping away flakes of it until she dug into the wood beneath. The platform swayed again as she tried to haul herself onto it. Temba, struggling in sudden panic to draw his knife, was being prevented by a branch behind him. Then another of the vital cords holding the platform to the tree snapped.

The whole thing sagged drunkenly and if Temba had not grabbed at a branch above his head he would have been thrown to the ground. The snow leopard screeched, and her claws rasped even more furiously as she also fought to keep from falling.

The strain was too much. Another cord snapped, and the flimsy platform collapsed. Temba yelled in terror. He reached up with his left hand to get a grip on something, but his fingers clutched at thin air. Unable to hold himself with one hand he swung outward and tried to leap clear of the tangle of loosely tied branches—wreckage of the platform—on the ground below him. The snow leopard had worked her way around to the other side of the tree and was still trying to get up to the place where Temba had been.

Temba was lucky. He broke his fall with two hands on a branch, but his right foot went through the platform wreckage and touched living flesh. It was the young goat, pinned down by the clutter of twigs and branches. But Temba, certain he had trod on the snow leopard, gave a shriek of terror and tried to jump clear before claws or fangs tore at his leg. There was no sound from the goat, for it had been completely winded when the wreckage of the platform fell on it.

The bravest man could have been forgiven for being frightened, and Temba Droma was not yet fourteen years of age. Struggling clear of the wreckage he ran for the compound, yelling for help. The terror in his voice halted the snow leopard. She had been about to scurry away, shocked by the sudden break-up of the platform and believing it another of the devil tricks of the two-legged creatures. It was the fear in the hill boy's voice that halted her.

Fear was something she could understand. She swiveled around to face the compound, heard the *thud-thud-thud* of Temba's feet and, realizing that he was running away from her, raced in pursuit. Had Temba not continued to yell the leopard might have been more cautious; but the terror in his voice told her that she need not be afraid of him and made her forget her own fears.

The rifle shot had wakened the sheep and goats and startled the pony. Shying from the baaing and bleating flock, the pony pranced and snorted until the Hindu grabbed it by the halter. Temba's appeals for help were drowned in the uproar.

"Hold the beast steady while I get this last load lashed on," the gunsmith urged. "Then I'll get away. You'll have to give yourself a bump on the head to show I knocked you out." Nasir Ali grinned maliciously at the thought.

The Hindu was too busy to worry over this attempt at humor. He was trying to hold the pony by the head, and at the same time keep an eye on the low place in the wall where he expected to see either Temba or the snow leopard appear. To add to his difficulties the pony was now working itself into a frenzy, plunging and kicking so that, heavily built man though the Hindu was, he found himself jerked this way and that by the animal's struggles.

Nasir Ali was swearing, for while the pony pranced he had no chance to lash the last load on its back. He was further hampered by the rifle he had loosely slung over his right shoulder. He was just about to lay it down when Temba Droma appeared. He leaped over the broken part of the wall like an Olympic hurdler—and only yards behind him was the snow leopard.

Temba scarcely saw Nasir Ali, who turned, dropped the bundle, and swung the rifle off his shoulder in one swift, smooth movement. And he scarcely saw the pony, which had its back to him and was plunging and kicking. Temba's one thought was to get to the far side of the fire so that the leaping flames might hold off the snow leopard until he had time to drag his long knife from its sheath. During his dash for the compound he had been too terrified—and there had been no time—to lay a hand on the handle, for his pursuer had been just behind his heels. Only her limp saved the young hill boy from death. Now she leaped onto the wall behind him but, unlike Temba, she did not immediately jump down into the compound.

Balanced on the wall, her rosette-spotted body shining guinea gold in the firelight, she would have struck terror into the heart of anyone. Her eyes were like little pools of purple flame; her jaws were wide, showing her gleaming fangs; and there was a frightening snarl in her drawn-back lips. When, after a moment's pause, she leaped off the wall into the compound there was a momentary flash of light on her forepaws that showed her unsheathed, curved, dagger-sharp claws.

In her anger and hunger, and with a victim so close, the snow leopard forgot her fear of the flames. But as she alighted, all four paws together, her body crouched and every muscle tensed for the next leap, she saw not one human, but three and, in addition, the strange shaggy-coated pony, rearing and kicking out as it tried to break away from the Hindu's restraining grip. For a moment the snow leopard was immobile. Her hesitation gave her enemies a chance to act.

Temba had reached the far side of the fire and was dragging his long knife from its sheath. Nasir Ali, forgetting in his excitement that his rifle was useless, was pushing a cartridge into the breech of the gun. The Hindu, his hands wet with sweat, was struggling to swing the pony around so that it would be between him and the snow leopard. But the pony, too, had seen the rosette-dotted figure poised on the wall and, though the Hindu was using every ounce of his weight and strength, he was not strong enough to hold the pony still.

With a terror-stricken neigh the shaggy-coated beast whirled around. Its thick and immensely powerful neck arched under the Hindu's weight. Like a bundle on the end of a string, the man was lifted off his feet and swung in an arc. The halter rope slipped through his sweating fingers, and he was thrown across the compound, his shriek lost in the pandemonium of baas and bleats from the sheep and goats. He fell and lay still. The freed pony whirled around and lashed out with his hind feet in a series of vicious kicks.

Temba, who had now drawn his long knife, saw the snow leopard leap, just as the pony dropped her head well down and lashed out again. With a soggy *thud* the unshod hooves took the snow leopard full in the chest. Temba saw her firelit body go hurtling backward like a curled-up ball, then come to rest a few yards from the motionless Hindu.

Nasir Ali had to leap for his life as the excited pony came charging toward him. Neighing shrilly, it dashed almost to the wall, wheeled back, swerved from the fire, then wheeled again.

"Quiet! Quiet! Q U I E T!" Nasir Ali roared. He managed to grab the halter in his left hand and drag the frightened pony to a stop. Then he slapped it across the cheek with the barrel of his rifle—a cruel blow, but one which did quiet the pony for a moment. Again he struck the pony. Then, ducking under its neck, he advanced cautiously toward the prostrate snow leopard.

The snow leopard was not unconscious. The pony's terrific kick in the ribs had driven all the air from her lungs, and she was struggling for breath, her chest heaving. But at the sight of the man advancing toward her she somehow managed to roll onto her side, and then onto her feet. She was getting her breath back, but it was too late. From a distance of no more than eight feet Nasir Ali coolly took aim and fired.

12
A Rifle for
a Man

THERE WAS A SHARP CLICK, BUT NO EXPLOSION; NO yard-long flame leaped from the muzzle. Too late, Nasir Ali remembered he had the rifle with the broken firing pin!

The click of the bolt going home stirred the snow leopard to action, and before the gunsmith could do anything, she was on him. Rising from a crouching position she landed with both forepaws on Nasir Ali's chest. He was already stepping backward, and the snow leopard's weight threw him completely off balance. With a roar of fear and rage he went down, his head and shoulders only a yard from the fire. He got his hands at the animal's throat in an effort to keep her fangs from him. He was a strong man, and fear gave him added strength; but the snow leopard was also strong, and she was as desperate as the man.

It was Temba who put an end to the battle. Swinging his big knife he screamed at the snow leopard. When she looked over her shoulder at him for an instant, he did the same thing he had done earlier—he swung his knife into the fire, sending fragments of burning wood scattering all about and a host of sparks flying into the air. Now the snow leopard turned from Nasir Ali and, desperation in her eyes, she faced the young hill boy. Again Temba swung his knife and shouted.

The snow leopard snarled, but did not retreat. Temba was on the opposite side of the fire. Kicking at what was left of the blaze, he sent one or two embers straight at the spotted hunter. She snarled defiance, then turned toward the huddle of sheep and goats standing by in terrified silence. This time she was not going to be cheated. She was too hungry.

She did not make another kill, for luckily the sheep and the goat she had killed earlier had been dropped carelessly on the ground, awaiting the time when Temba could skin and cut up the carcasses. The hunter grabbed the goat and, glaring at Temba, limped to the wall, scrambled over it, and was gone.

For perhaps five seconds Temba stood and stared at the spot as if unable to believe his luck. In a little over five minutes he had fallen out of his tree platform, been chased by the snow leopard, had seen Nasir Ali go down with the hunter's fangs at his throat, and then had himself driven her away. Now she had gone. She had taken a dead goat, to be sure, but the price was cheap. For once the good spirits had helped him.

The frantic pony brought Temba to his senses. Nasir Ali's blow had temporarily quieted the beast, but now it

was again rushing backward and forward, occasionally
pausing to lash out with its hind hooves and threatening
at any moment to trample to death one or more of the
flock.

Nasir Ali was painfully trying to raise himself into a
sitting position. The front of his coat showed a spreading
stain of blood. The frantic movements of the frightened
pony made Temba decide that his first task was to tether
the beast before it did more damage. It took him five
minutes to bring the pony under control. That done,
Temba went to look at the Hindu, a huddled figure
propped against the wall. Feeling he owed more to him
than to Nasir Ali, Temba gently dragged the limp figure
nearer to the fire. The Hindu was groaning a little, but
there seemed no sign of a wound, so Temba turned to do
what he could for Nasir Ali.

The gunsmith had dragged himself to a sitting position, and Temba propped him up with some of their bales
of merchandise. Then he looked at the man's wounds.
The dagger-sharp claws had raked Nasir Ali's chest, missing his throat by inches. A man less tough than this gunsmith would certainly have fainted from shock and loss
of blood.

Remembering what the *memsahib* had said about claw
wounds, Temba smeared what was left of the penicillin
paste into the gashes. Then he used up the rest of the
lint, binding it in place with Nasir Ali's turban.

Though in much pain, it was beneath the dignity of
the man to do more than wince while Temba was bandaging him. When the task was finished he startled Temba

by a throaty chuckle and a remark. "I laugh because this is the first time I have ever known a snow leopard, or any kind of leopard, to befriend a boy. You should reward the beast with the other carcass. She saved you, boy; saved you." Then, as if the effort of speaking had been too much, his eyes closed and his face was contorted in pain.

"Saved me?" Temba had no idea what the man meant. "How could a leopard save me? She has almost killed my father; she has killed several of our flock; yet you say she has saved me. Saved me from what?"

Nasir Ali opened his eyes again. "She saved you from me," he murmured, "and from that cunning limb of *shaitan*, the Hindu. We were going to rob you. Is he dead?"

"No, I don't think so," Temba said, turning to look again at the moaning Hindu. "I do not know what is wrong with him. There is no bleeding that I can see."

"It would be wrong if he lives and I die," Nasir Ali snarled venomously. "Look, boy, bring me that rifle, and I will . . ."

"Bring you the rifle!" Temba said sharply. "I bring *you* no rifle. You just said you are a thief. You might shoot me."

Nasir Ali's shoulders sagged against the bundles of merchandise. He looked at Temba for a few moments, then nodded wearily. "Yes, I am a thief," he said. "But I would not shoot you, not now. For if I am to live, I must keep you alive. No one else could carry me to the white woman doctor at Rakfazar Bazaar. That is what I want you to do for me. Listen, and I will tell you what that cunning Hindu planned. You think him a friend, but he is a bigger enemy than I ever was."

Anxious that he should not take all the blame, Nasir Ali told Temba the whole story of how the Hindu had planned to rob him and his father of their goods, their flocks, and their precious rifle. He ended with a plea: "When the new day comes, you must find the other rifle —the one you left behind at the tree where the goat was tethered. That will shoot straight, and you must have a rifle. The snow leopard will come back."

Temba closed his eyes in despair as he thought of the wicked scheme which had almost worked, of the rifle, and of the young goat he had left lying at the foot of the tree. Yet to go back now to see if it was still alive and to hunt for the rifle would, he knew, be madness. He looked at Nasir Ali. Exhausted, he had lain back again, his eyes closed.

A long, drawn-out groan from the Hindu, who was now regaining consciousness, brought Temba's attention to his other enemy. He had suffered a very hard knock on the head when he was hurled against the wall. What was more, his left collarbone was broken. Temba had no idea how to treat a concussion or a broken bone, so he made the Hindu as comfortable as he could and, after looking at his sleeping father, sat down to wait for the new day.

Toward dawn Nasir Ali tried to get to his knees. He had been awake for some time and had decided that if he could overpower Temba he might still get out of trouble by stealing the pony and riding it down to Rakfazar

Bazaar. He made a determined effort, but he was too weak. After getting to his knees he collapsed. Temba, who had been catnapping, heard him and woke immediately. He helped the gunsmith back to a more comfortable position, then fanned the dying fire to new life.

Using melted snow he made a kettle of strong tea and thickened it liberally with barley meal. Filling a mug he knelt by his father's side and gently shook him, calling him by his name. To his delight Shainu Droma stirred, blinked, then opened his eyes. He did not speak to Temba, but he took the mug and drained it. Then he asked for a second mugful. Temba could see that he was much better. And so he was, for the penicillin had killed the infection in his leg and the antibiotic tablets had lowered his temperature. After the second mugful of tea he even smiled at Temba.

As the two injured men drank the tea Temba gave them, the Hindu groaned continually. He pleaded with Temba to take him down to Rakfazar Bazaar at once. "I will pay you well," he croaked. "All I have is yours if I can only be taken to the *memsahib*. If I do not get help from her very soon I shall die."

"And die you should," Nasir Ali snarled impatiently. "Go for the rifle, boy, before the leopard returns."

Temba, knowing now that he could not trust either of these men, tied his knife to a length of bamboo and, with this as his only weapon, left the compound. The sun was just peeping over the snow-clad peaks. It was very quiet, for at these heights even the ravens only came occasionally, and no insects droned until midsummer.

When he was about twenty yards from the tree a queer sound broke the brooding quiet. Temba stopped, and his thoughts went at once to the snow leopard. There was plenty of cover for her among the scattered boulders. His heart was thumping as he looked anxiously around, but he could see no sign of movement. He was sixty yards from the safety of the compound, on the path where the snow leopard had almost caught him the night before.

After a minute of tense waiting he could endure the silence no longer. He gave a loud yell, hoping to scare the snow leopard from her hiding place. Within seconds the answer came—an unexpected answer, the pathetic bleating of a goat. *Aaaa-aaa-aaah!*

Temba could hardly believe his ears. The little goat staked at the foot of the tree was still alive! Cautiously he approached the tree. There was a movement under the wreckage of the platform. The young goat was pinned down by the branches, and further held by the rope about its neck. At the same moment Temba saw the rifle. Grabbing it, he immediately reloaded. Now he felt better. If the accursed snow leopard came again he could kill her. There would be no hasty shooting this time, he promised himself.

He lifted the wreckage of the platform. When he cut the rope that still tethered the young goat, it scampered about him like a puppy, bleating joyously.

"You shall live until you are an old nanny," Temba told it, stroking its dusty back. "A good spirit has been looking after both you and me, for we have seen Death staring at us, and not felt the touch of his cold hands."

He turned back toward the compound, the goat bleating and scampering about, too overjoyed at its release
even to snatch at a mouthful of the thin grass. When he
had gone a dozen yards Temba paused and looked again
toward the edge of the cliff. Now that he had a rifle he
could face the snow leopard on more than equal terms.
And if he were lucky, he might even be able to pick her
off without her seeing him.

Quietly he approached the edge of the cliff, dropped to
one knee, and looked over. For a moment the narrow
strip of land between the river and the bottom of the cliff
seemed empty, then he saw something move. It was a
snow-leopard kitten. Even as he watched, the mother
came in sight and dropped another kitten by the side of
the first. Then she vanished, only to return again with her
third kitten. Then she lay and began to lick them as they
fed in the sunshine.

Temba eased his rifle over the edge of the cliff. He
would not miss at this range. The distance was no more
than sixty feet, and his target was lying almost motionless
in the bright sunshine. As he took first pressure on the
trigger the young goat began to nibble at his right heel.
Temba kicked impatiently, but the goat was in the mood
for play and returned, bleating joyously. "Go away,"
Temba ordered, thrusting the goat away with his foot.

When Temba turned and pointed the rifle down the
cliff face again there had been a change. The snow leopard must have heard him, for she was on her feet looking
up. Her pale gold body, with its black rosette markings
was glossy in the morning sun. She was a perfect target

in Temba's gunsight, unmoving and beautiful as a wild mother can be. She must have decided that Temba was too far away to harm her or the kittens, for she yawned and lay down. At once her kittens hungrily resumed their feeding.

Again Temba took first pressure on the trigger, and lined up his sights for a heart shot. Now it needed the merest tightening of his forefinger to send a bullet into the sunlit body below. He held his breath, as a good marksman does before firing. At that moment one of the kittens moved and covered the spot where the bullet would have gone. Temba eased the pressure on the trigger.

For several seconds he stared down. "I ought to kill you," he whispered. "Your skin would fetch plenty of rupees in the market at Rakfazar Bazaar, and yet if you die the kittens will die." He shook his head as if not sure what to do. Then he whispered, "One doesn't kill babies."

He knew he ought to kill the snow leopard. She had been a costly nuisance to them, and might well be a nuisance to other caravaners. Yet the thought of the three kittens, now beginning to romp about their mother, made him finally draw back from the edge of the cliff.

"Next year," he promised himself, "there may be no kittens. Then if I see you, you *will* die!" For some reason he could not explain, he felt happy as he walked back to the compound. It was a strange feeling, but he liked it.

For the next two days Temba nursed the three men and took care of the remaining sheep and goats. The Hindu kept trying to persuade him to help him onto the pony and take him down to the *memsahib*. He promised a hatful of rupees if Temba would do this, and only stopped his urging when Nasir Ali finally threatened to cut his throat if he did not cease his whining.

Shainu Droma was now sleeping much less and eating with greater appetite. After drinking his tea one morning he called his son to him and asked what had been happening, and why these two men were lying in their camp. Temba told him the whole story, while the Hindu and Nasir Ali watched in frightened silence. To their relief, when the youngster had finished, Shainu said, "Take the sheep this snow leopard has killed and throw it over the cliff as near to her lair as you can. It is a fair price to pay, if she will let our flock graze in peace."

While Temba was carrying the dead sheep to the edge of the cliff, Shainu Droma spoke to the two injured men. "So two men planned to cheat a boy and rob a wounded man! I think there will be plenty of time for you to think over what you tried to do to me and my son, for there is only one pony, and as I will not be able to walk for a few days, I shall be riding the pony."

Nasir Ali said nothing, but the Hindu pleaded and finally wept in terror.

"Did you weep when you planned to rob me?" Shainu Droma asked sternly.

When Temba returned, he reported that the carcass had fallen near the snow leopard's lair.

"She will get it, my Father," he said.

"If she leaves us in peace, then I am satisfied," Shainu said.

Each day the Hindu pleaded for mercy and promised all kinds of rewards if he could be taken to Rakfazar

Bazaar, but Nasir Ali, whose wounds were now growing worse, said nothing.

On the third day Shainu Droma said he felt strong enough to ride the pony. While the Hindu again wept and pleaded for mercy, Temba helped his father onto the pony, then led it and their remaining sheep and goats down the track.

Three miles down the hill he halted at a convenient spot. He helped his father off the pony, made him as comfortable as he could, and then returned to the compound with the pony.

The Hindu was almost hysterical with fear when Temba helped Nasir Ali onto the pony. The gunsmith, whose wounds were already showing the ominous signs of blood poisoning, looked at the hill boy and managed a grin. "You can hurt men like him two ways, boy," he muttered. "By taking their money or by frightening them. This poor fool has never been hurt like this before. It is a lesson he will remember for a long time."

The journey down to Rakfazar Bazaar took three tiring days, for Temba and the pony carried the injured trio down in relays. After carrying Shainu Droma a mile or so, Temba would put him down and go back for Nasir Ali, and then again for the Hindu.

When they finally reached the village Nasir Ali was taken immediately to the *memsahib*'s tent, for he was now suffering severely from blood poisoning. As they drew near the tent, the gunsmith fumbled in his coat for his big leather purse. With much difficulty he opened it and from it took a key. Gruffly, he said to Temba, "We who saw first light in the Khyber Pass swear to take a life for a life, but we also remember our friends. Take this key, boy. It is for the big box in my workshop. The rifle in it is yours as payment for my life."

The Hindu offered no payment when he was carried to the *memsahib*'s tent. He was feeling too sorry for himself to think of anyone else.

Shainu Droma's wounds were healing. He did not need to see the *memsahib*. He needed only time and rest.

Temba took his father through the street of Rakfazar Bazaar, still busy with buyers and sellers of goods. On the *maidan* they found the rest of their sheep and goats and Shar, their remaining mastiff, waiting. They paid the hill woman who had fed and watered the flock and settled down in their newly made camp.

The story of what had happened up in the pass went around Rakfazar Bazaar like wildfire, and many of Shainu Droma's acquaintances came to see him. Among them was an old, bearded man, Ghulam Ali, the man Temba thought was dead. He drank tea with them, while Temba stared and wondered. He had never doubted the news the Hindu had given him that Ghulam Ali had died of the quick death—cholera.

Ghulam Ali proved to be the kind of friend Temba's father had said he was. He helped Temba find a gunsmith to fix his father's rifle. He sold the goods they had brought in, and took Temba along to the various stalls in the bazaar to buy the things that would delight the hearts of his mother and sister. Ghulam Ali saw to it that no man cheated the young hill boy. For his own delight,

Temba was allowed to buy twelve large-headed copper nails and a new purse.

By the time the Rakfazar Bazaar was coming to an end Shainu Droma's leg wounds were healed sufficiently for him to begin hobbling about with the aid of a stick, and the three of them drank tea with many of their old friends.

Before they began their return journey, Temba visited the *memsahib* again. This time he marched boldly to her tent. Eyes gleaming, he laid on the table his new purse of untanned leather. Untying the thong he upturned the purse and shook out sixteen jingling rupees. "These," he said proudly, "are in payment for the life of Shainu Droma. Today he walks with only a limp." He pushed the coins toward the white woman, lifted his hands in salute, and was gone. It was a moment Temba would never forget, for until then he had never been allowed to settle a debt. He felt he was very near to being a man.

Half an hour later Temba and his father and Shar and the flock were on their way back to the pass. That night they camped again in the rough-walled compound. They started their fire and cooked their mutton and made their tea by the light of a waning moon. The mighty Himalayan peaks shimmered in the cold white light, and there was a crispness in the air that both father and son enjoyed. The warmth, dust, and smells of Rakfazar Bazaar were something they had been glad to leave behind.

Before they moved off the next morning, Temba went to the edge of the cliff and looked down, drawn by a strange desire to see the snow leopard once more. The river had ceased to rush along. The first flood of water from melting snow was already far down in the plains of India.

At first there was no sign of life. Then, just as Temba was about to turn away, a snow-leopard kitten came in sight. It moved to the water's edge and stood staring across. A few moments later it was joined by a second kitten, and then by the last of the trio. All stared intently across the stream to the valley. Temba followed the direction of their gaze and saw the mother.

If she was limping it was scarcely noticeable. She must have gone hunting with the first light of day, and she must have been able to run and leap with almost her usual speed and stealth, for in her jaws was one of the wild blue *bharal* from the upper slopes. She splashed across at a point where the river ran no deeper than an inch or so, and the kittens were all over her the moment she put down her prize.

"I could kill you easily," Temba murmured, lifting his rifle and staring through the sights. But the safety catch was on, and his finger did not even stray to the trigger. He stared at his "target" for perhaps a minute, then obeyed a shout from his father calling him back to the compound where everything was packed and the caravan was ready to move on.

That night they camped at fourteen thousand feet, in a tent that quivered and shook under the icy blasts of the wind. They rose early, drank their strong black tea, and moved on again. There was a mist cap of snow blowing from the top of the nearest peak; the icy walls of a precipice almost a thousand feet deep were pale blue in the morning sun. Everywhere there was breathtaking beauty, but neither father nor son noticed it. Three days' journey would take them to Temba's mother and sister, who would be waiting anxiously for the reunion.

For Temba, this morning was different from any other, because his father had motioned for him to lead the caravan. Temba spoke no words, but his shoulders went a little squarer and his chin lifted. To be allowed to lead the caravan meant that his father now looked on him as a *man*. The driving wind carried stinging hail with it, but the hill boy scarcely lowered his head. Slung over his right shoulder was a Lee-Enfield rifle, the weapon he had taken from Nasir Ali's big box. Temba had burnished it with oil until it gleamed. In his pocket were the copper nails he would drive into the butt during the summer months. The nails would be an ornament, but they would also show that Temba Droma was now a *man*!

The wind brought mist with it, a low cloud that swallowed them gradually. First came the boy with the rifle and the proud look on his face, then the sheep and goats with their panniers, watched over by Shar. Last of all came Shainu Droma, limping just a little. All were satisfied; they were back in their own hills.

Down the pass, on the other side of the mountain, the snow leopard lay contentedly in the morning sun. Her ribs no longer showed like sticks through her glossy hide. Her kittens played about her. She had no thoughts of men or gunshot sounds or flashes of fire. There were wild sheep on the upper slopes, and her paw was healed. She could hunt again!